Murder, London-Australia

MURDER,

LONDON-AUSTRALIA

John Creasey

CHARLES SCRIBNER'S SONS
New York

CONTENTS

1

OLD FRIEND?

"Where's he from?" asked Roger West.

"He's an Australian," Kebble answered.

"Australia's a big place. What part does he come from?"

In a way, the question was cruel. Kebble's blue eyes clouded, his lips tightened, for a moment he made Roger think he was going to snap back a retort. That would be a pity. It was late afternoon, it had been a busy day, Kebble was pleased with himself—he was too often, that was his chief weakness—and it was a bad time to have to discipline a sergeant in the Criminal Investigation Department.

"Anything else you need to know about him?" Kebble's question fell just short of being sarcastic.

Roger, who didn't know the sergeant well, now tested him for both good humour and a sense of humour.

"Everything!" He grinned. "Age, appearance, colour of eyes, accent if any, general appearance such as breadline or in the prosperity stakes. You know. The lot."

Kebble was almost laughing by the time the recital was over—a good sign.

"I won't be long," he promised, and walked out of the office.

Roger pushed his chair back and stood up. He was a big, powerful man, good looking enough to have been called 'Handsome' in his early days at the Yard, and the nickname had stuck. Now his wavy blond hair was streaked with grey, but the overall impression was fair and youthful. He moved with a positive, almost aggressive briskness, and often talked in the same way.

He had risen from the ranks to very near the top.

This was a small room but a room more suitable to a Chief Superintendent of the C.I.D. might have more space, but would not command a view over the Thames Embankment as this did. There were other advantages to a small room; somehow it made formality more difficult.

Kebble was today's stand-in for Cope, the Chief Inspector who usually shared the office. It was a pity about Cope. He was ill, seriously ill, and the hospital reports weren't good. He would probably get just well enough to retire early on a pension smaller than he really needed; bad luck, at fifty-one.

Kebble was thirty-two. He had been transferred from one of the divisions on the perimeter of the Metropolitan Police District, one of the superior residential areas. According to his record, he was a bright boy. To reach the top at the Yard one had to have a lot of luck as well as intelligence and skill, however; memory played a more important part than most realized, too. Kebble was certainly having the luck; three men off duty, through sickness, one by accident, two on all day court work, so Detective Sergeant Kebble was sitting-in as chief assistant to one of the Yard's senior officers.

Roger picked up the photograph of a girl and carried it to the window. She was pretty, even in death. It was a good thing the picture did not show her neck.

What turned men into stranglers?

Who was this girl?

It was a puzzle, but not yet a worrying one; yesterday morning she had been found in the back room of a cheap boarding-house, choked to death. Roger West, who had seen her in the morgue, could picture the dark bruises on her neck. He hadn't the pathologist's final report yet, but death by strangulation seemed a safe bet.

The morning newspapers had published this picture, with the caption:

"DO YOU KNOW THIS GIRL?"

If so, please communicate with New Scotland Yard, Whitehall 1212, or with your nearest police station.

The man who Kebble felt sure was Australian was not the first who claimed to know her, but none of the many others who had responded had really been able to help. According to them she had seventeen different names and came from a dozen different parts of England.

There was a tap at the door.

"Come in."

Roger turned his head as Kebble entered. There was something sinewy about him, about his rather long neck with its prominent Adam's apple, and bony wrists. His eyes were as alert as a bird's. In fact, he looked vaguely like a turkey.

"What else do we know now?" Roger inquired.

"The man's name is Benjamin Limm—L-I-double M—he comes from a place called Cowra in New South Wales," deposed Kebble. "He is a sheep farmer, aged about thirty-five, widower, five-eleven, lean, hardy-looking, grey-eyed, and fair-haired."

Kebble was poker-faced when he stopped.

Roger called it a day as far as ribbing sergeants was concerned.

"Thanks. Do you think he knows our girl?"

"He says he's positive. He travelled from Australia on a cargo ship with her, and there were only nine passengers. He says this girl is Denise Morrison, who was travelling with her sister, Doreen. He doesn't seem to have any doubts at all."

"How long ago was this?" Roger asked.

"Four weeks since they landed at Southampton, ten since they left Melbourne," answered Kebble.

"I'll see this chap," Roger said. "I'll ask him the stock questions, too, including those you've asked. Take everything down."

Kebble nodded.

"Go get him," Roger said.

As Kebble stalked out of the office Roger studied that picture again. How old was she? Twenty-two? Twenty-three? No more, anyhow. Dark-haired, a little too thin except at the breast, where she was heavy; *had been heavy,* he corrected himself. He felt uneasy, and that was not a good sign. Thirty years at the Yard—well, nearly thirty—gave one a kind of prescience which the Press liked to call a sixth sense. Every now and again it made itself felt, as it did now, and as it had since the investigation into this crime began. Until this moment he had not allowed himself to admit it, but now the feeling was too strong to be ignored.

Denise Morrison, who had a sister——

There was a brisk, almost peremptory tap at the door, and Kebble appeared.

"Shall I bring Mr. Limm in, sir?"

"Please."

Kebble's description had been good, but missed one important factor: vitality. Limm came striding in, a lean, rangy man with a glint of impatience in his eyes. He was good looking in a lean, long-jawed way, the kind who would probably attract youngish women.

Roger, standing at his desk, held out a hand.

"Mr. Limm, I'm glad to see you. Thank you for taking the trouble to come to us about this bad business."

Limm's handshake was quick, his hand cool.

"Bad business?" he echoed. "How bad?"

"Don't you know?"

"No, Superintendent, I don't. I saw that photograph in a newspaper, and I came to say I knew Denise Morrison. Is she——" He broke off.

Roger said, quietly: "She's dead, Mr. Limm."

Limm echoed: *"Dead."* All the vitality seemed to be drained out of him. *"Dead?"* he repeated, making it a question as if his reason rejected the truth. "Oh, no."

"I'm afraid it's true. Push up a chair for Mr. Limm, Sergeant."

Kebble was at hand with an upright chair. Limm dropped into it. The glint of impatience had gone, only shock revealed itself in his eyes and his body. He sat staring at Roger.

"How well did you know her?" Roger asked.

"Er—not so well," Limm answered. Then he squared his shoulders and his voice strengthened. "As well as you get to know a fellow passenger on a six weeks sea trip. I suppose that's knowing her well." He hesitated, as if there was something he wanted to say but either couldn't get it out or didn't know how to put it. "Poor kid. Dead. She was so——"

He raised his hands and let them drop on to his knees.

"Full of life," he finished. "Absolutely full of life. She— how did she die?"

"We think she was murdered," Roger said very clearly.

Limm caught his breath, formed the word 'no' again but did not utter it. Over at his desk now, Kebble was busy with his notes. Outside, traffic seemed very close to the open windows, the occasional roar of an engine changing gear drowned all sounds in this office.

"Mr. Limm, did you know Denise Morrison before you joined the ship?"

"No," Limm said. "No, I didn't."

"Are you sure her name was Denise Morrison?"

After a pause, Limm said flatly: "Yes, I'm sure." He squared his shoulders, and some life seemed to seep back into him. "I saw her passport. She was on the passenger list, too."

"Do you know where she came from? And what she did?"

"A town called Dandenong, not far from Melbourne," Limm answered. "She worked in a dress shop, did some modelling, and the buying. She went to the Melbourne and Sydney houses every season to stock up. Doreen was secretary to a big garage. They'd been saving up for years for this trip." Limm's tone was husky, as if his memory of the dead girl was hurting him. He became suddenly aggressive. "Have you any reason to think she didn't tell the truth or gave a false name?"

"I'm trying to make sure of her identity," Roger said mildly.

"You can be sure all right," Limm said gruffly. "If I wasn't certain I wouldn't say so."

"You should certainly know a girl who's been a fellow passenger for six weeks," Roger agreed. "But that isn't legal evidence, of course. Identification from a photograph never satisfies a coroner."

"Coroner?"

"There has to be an inquest, and I'm afraid we'll need your testimony, unless we can find someone else who knew her better," Roger explained. "The inquest isn't likely to be delayed very long. Can you find time?"

Limm said with a growl in his voice: "If I have to, I have to. What are you really telling me, Superintendent?"

"I would like you to see the body."

Limm's lips were set very tightly until he asked in a clipped tone: "Why me?"

"We haven't yet found anyone else who knows her."

"What about her sister?"

"We've heard nothing from any sister."

"Does she know——" Limm began, only to break off as if in astonishment. "You mean you don't know where Doreen is?"

"We didn't even know she existed." Roger stood up and moved slowly towards the window. "The body—Denise—was found yesterday morning by the landlady of a boarding-house in South Kensington. She had registered as Mrs. Brown—was she married?" As he flashed that question, Roger spun round.

"Not—not as far as I know."

"Was she engaged?"

"Not as far as I know," Limm repeated. "Superintendent, just tell me the whole story, will you? Don't jump about so much—— I want to understand the situation properly."

Kebble glanced up at Roger, with a near grin.

"I can't tell you the whole story because I don't know it," Roger replied. "But I'll tell you what we do know. She had given her name as Mrs. Brown. She said she was expecting her husband to arrive later. The landlady heard her go out about nine o'clock on the night of her death. She came back after midnight with a man whom no one saw, as far as we yet know. No one heard the man leave. At ten o'clock in the morning the landlady went to see if the young woman wanted anything. She was lying on her back, in her nightdress, dead."

Limm was twisting round in his chair and watching Roger closely; he didn't speak.

"That is all and everything we know about the girl you call Denise Morrison and who called herself Brown. She may have been really married for all we know. She wore a brass wedding ring."

"*Brass?*"

Roger moved to his desk and picked up a small plastic bag, tied at the neck, and labelled. Inside was a ring which looked as if it could have been made of gold for the plastic dulled the brashness of the brass.

"Except for her clothes, everything else had been taken away."

"*Everything?*"

"Handbag, money—if she had any—make-up, the lot. She had a new dacron-and-wool suit, made by the tens of thousands, new shoes, new stockings. Her girdle and brassière were old—our experts here haven't yet identified the place of origin or manufacture. There's our problem, Mr. Limm—to find a man we believe to be a murderer, and to find out why this young woman was murdered." He spun round. "Did you ever get the impression that she was frightened of anything?"

"Frightened?" echoed Limm. "That girl didn't know the meaning of fear. She and her sister had saved every penny they could for this trip. They were going to work where they could, hitch-hike through England and then the Continent. She had so much courage it almost scared me." He stood up. "If anything frightened her, it was something that happened after she reached England. I'll stake my reputation on that."

"Did she tell you who she was going to see in England?"

"No," Limm answered. "I took it for granted she didn't

know anyone. Three years ago her mother died—the father had been dead for a long time. They had no relatives in Australia, and as far as they knew none in England." Limm began to walk about the room. "This is the most awful thing I've ever heard of." He stopped in front of Roger. "Her sister— that's the part I can't believe. Doreen worshipped Denise, she was like a watchdog. She was the practical one, held the money, carried out the plans, Denise made the plans, then left everything to her sister. Denise was the good-looker, too, but Doreen had the brains. Wherever Denise was, Doreen wouldn't be far behind. Believe me, you've got to find Doreen."

"Have you a photograph of her?" Roger asked.

Kebble's sniff seemed to reject this question as absurd.

Limm put his hand to his pocket, took out a wallet, thumbed through it, and stopped at some snapshots. He took these out; there were seven or eight, all quite small.

"It's not much good but it's all I've got," he said. "One of the passengers took it and sent me a copy."

There were nine people in the photograph, including Limm. One was undoubtedly the dead girl; another, smaller girl stood next to her, a young couple and an elderly couple, and one man in officer's uniform. Roger went to his desk and picked up a magnifying glass. It was a good picture and the faces would enlarge well.

"What can you tell me about the other passengers?" Roger asked.

Limm hesitated.

"There was Doreen, of course. Then there were the Donellis, an elderly couple going overseas for the first time since they emigrated about thirty years ago. They own some cafés in Adelaide. Kept themselves to themselves. Then there were Jack and Jill Parrish, honeymooners although they never admitted it. He's a Queensland banana grower, she's English —she'd been out to see some relations at Surfers Paradise."

"Where's that?" asked Roger.

"It's a holiday hot-spot on the South Queensland coast—part of the Gold Coast, you must have heard of that." Roger didn't say so, but he hadn't. "There was Perce Sheldon, an insurance broker, he did the trip for his health." Limm almost leered. "He ate enough for two. Except for old Sam Hackett, that's the lot. Liveliest near-octogenarian I ever met, Sam was. Looked like a piece of twisted gum root after a forest fire. He said he'd made his money in pearls and mother-of-pearl before the trade collapsed up on the West Coast."

Limm obviously knew his Australia.

"Very comprehensive—many thanks," Roger said. "May I borrow this photograph?"

"So long as you mean borrow."

"My word on it."

"I'll accept that." Limm smiled almost freely for the first time since he had been told of Denise Morrison's death. "Will you look for Doreen?"

"Her description will be put on general call before I go home tonight," Roger promised.

"You're right," Limm said. His grin appeared again but was short-lived. "I don't understand them breaking up, and I don't understand why Doreen didn't get in touch with the police the minute she saw that photograph. It doesn't make sense." He seemed to square his shoulders again. "Didn't you say you wanted me to see Denise?"

Limm obviously steeled himself to show no emotion when the girl's face was uncovered in that chill, brightly lit morgue. Roger watched intently from across the bench, Kebble by Limm's side.

Abruptly, Roger pulled the sheet down to the bare shoulders, to show the bruised neck. Limm's composure broke. He clenched his teeth and clenched his hands.

Someone had clenched strong hands round that girl's throat not very long ago.

"For God's sake find Doreen," he said hoarsely.

Doreen Morrison was only about three miles away. She was asleep in a small, ill-furnished room, alone on a divan bed. She breathed so softly that she hardly seemed to be breathing at all. Had her eyes been open, the pin-point pupils would have betrayed the fact that she had been drugged with morphine.

2

SECOND WITNESS

LIMM had gone from Roger West's office.

Kebble had finished his notes; he would type them or have them typed in the morning. It was now nearly six o'clock, but he did not give the impression that he was fidgeting to be off. He had not asked Roger's opinion, and so shown considerable restraint. Roger finished signing some letters, rang for a messenger, and, as the man went out with the post, looked across at Kebble.

"What did you make of Limm?"

Kebble looked up quickly.

"Can't see any reason for suspecting he knows more than he said."

"Think he does?" asked Roger.

Kebble ventured: "I thought you thought he did."

"Not yet," Roger said. "I simply think he might, on the principle that we can't rule anyone out." He went on as if speaking to himself. "We're not allowed to presume guilt so why should we presume innocence?" He hoped that didn't sound as pretentious as it seemed to him. "Now, we've a lot to do. Any special date tonight?"

"No, sir."

"Good." Roger stretched out for the telephone, speaking as

he did so. "Take that snapshot up to *Photography*, have enlargements done of all the faces, get the prints of the Morrison sisters sent round to all Divisions and Home Counties tonight." Into the telephone he said: "Get my wife, please." He put the receiver down and went on to Kebble without a pause. "Find out from the shipping company where the S.S. *Kookaburra* is now. If she's in London, check with the Port police and Thames Division—I'd like to see the captain and the crew. If she's not in London, find out where she is. Then get a full passenger list, with the English addresses of all passengers who landed at Southampton—any British port, for that matter."

His telephone bell rang.

"Got all that?"

"I think so," Kebble said.

Roger's hand hovered impatiently over the telephone. "*Think?*"

"Yes, I have."

"Get things started, then come and see me again." Roger lifted the telephone. "West.... Oh, put him through...." His tone changed but he was still brisk. "Hallo, Scoop, is Mum out?"

Kebble, disappearing through the door, was looking round at him.

"Hi, Dad," said Martin-called-Scoop, Roger's elder son. "Yes, she's gone over to Mrs. Pollisters, to some cocktail party or other. She said she would be back by seven, though."

"Tell her I may not be back until late," Roger said. "Had a good day?"

"Pretty good. I finished that painting of the newspaper boy. I think it's all right."

"Try painting a millionaire," said Roger. "He'd be more likely to buy his portrait."

"Never heard of art for art's sake?" asked Martin, with a hint of laughter in his voice.

"Try living on it," retorted Roger. "How's Fish?"

Martin chuckled. "He's in a hell of a stew. He's got the inside out of that old M.G. and can't find one of the pistons or something. He's sulphurous."

"Don't make him feel any worse," Roger cautioned.

"I won't get the chance. Dad——?"

"Yes?"

"What's on?"

"Bad men up to no good," Roger said bluffly.

"Don't put me off. Is it that girl? I mean the one whose photograph was in the *Globe* this morning?"

It was always a delicate matter to know how much to tell his sons, and how much to discourage them in their natural curiosity, but there was no point in hedging over this.

"Yes," Roger said simply.

"It's a damned shame."

"That's putting it mildly."

"I mean, a pretty girl like that."

"Don't judge entirely from looks," Roger said automatically. "Scoop, I really must go. Don't forget to tell Mum."

He rang off, and paused to look at Denise Morrison's photograph, trying to imagine how she would appear to a youth of twenty. 'A damned shame.' That summed up Scoop; his quick involvement in other people's affairs, and his ready sympathy despite an outward show of toughness. What would he say if he knew about the so far silent sister?

Roger put his son out of his mind, made some notes on a pad, then lifted the telephone.

"I'll be out of the office for five minutes," he said.

"Very good, sir."

Roger went along the nearer passage and up a flight of stairs, moving with controlled haste, a sign of tension, an indication of the vitality always in him; he could never get anywhere or do any job quickly enough for his own liking. He reached a sergeants' room, the one where Kebble should be, by rights. A man was talking on the telephone. As Roger drew nearer, he said:

"Don't blame me, Kitty, blame his devotion to duty.... All right, all right! Blame my new Boss, the great Handsome West.... Yes, West.... Kitty," the man went on in almost horrified tones, "that's as near sacrilege as you can get about anyone at Scotland Yard." He laughed. "Stay in and be good for once."

He rang off.

Roger, who wanted to send a sergeant to check on Benjamin Limm, walked past the partly open door without glancing in. So Kebble had lied about not having a date, a strong point in his favour. Roger soon turned back, to find two sergeants sitting on stools in front of old-fashioned high desks; they slid off almost to attention.

"Who's not busy?" Roger inquired, amiably.

One of the men, a short, almost dapper man named Scott, gave a one-sided smile.

"I've nothing that can't wait, sir."

"Good. Here's all I can tell you about the man Limm, who came to see me just now." Roger handed over some of the notes. "Check the address he gave, how long he's been there, get anything you can about him—all very discreetly. Understood?"

"Yes, sir!"

"Call me as soon as you can," Roger said. "I'll be in my office until eight o'clock at least. If I've gone by the time you've a report to make, call me at my house."

"I'll do that," promised Scott.

Roger nodded and went out. As he neared his own office the telephone was ringing incessantly, yet he had told the operator that he would be out, and operators seldom slipped up. With his natural kind of restrained haste, he opened the door, stretched across, and picked up the telephone.

"Yes?"

"Oh, Mr. West, I know you said you'd be out, but I've a man on the line who says he has to catch a plane in five minutes but wants a word with the officer in charge of the girl's photograph case."

"Thanks," Roger said. "I'll talk to him."

There was hardly a pause before the man came on the line. The first obvious thing was that his voice resembled Limm's, in the sense that the pronunciation of vowels was different from normal English. Over the telephone it sounded loud and harsh, not at all like Limm's.

"Are you handling the inquiry about the girl whose photo is in the *Globe*?"

It had been in all the newspapers except *The Times*; it was surprising how often the *Globe* was mentioned.

"I can tell you who she is," the man stated.

"Are you sure?"

"My word, yes. They don't come like Denise Morrison very often. I sailed from Australia on the same ship, the S.S. *Kookaburra*. Yes, sir, I'm sure. She was with her sister, Doreen. Superintendent, she's not in any trouble, is she?"

"I'm afraid she is," Roger said quietly.

"That's bad. I wish I hadn't got to go, but I had just three months sick leave, and if I'm not home by Wednesday *I'll* be in trouble. My name's Sheldon, Superintendent, Perce Sheldon. I'm from Adelaide in South Australia—insurance is my racket. Let me know if I can help, won't you?"

"Yes," Roger said. "What flight are you going on?"

"Flight 107 from London Airport," said Sheldon. "They're calling it right now. I hope Denise isn't in too much trouble. She was a beaut of a girl to have on board ship."

He banged down his receiver.

Roger put his down almost as quickly, made several notes before hearing footsteps outside; Kebble had been a long time in *Photography* but he might have stopped somewhere else on the way. He was frowning as the door closed behind him with a snap, pushed harder than was necessary.

Roger finished his notes.

"What's the trouble?"

"Missed 'em by five minutes," Kebble said gloomily.

"Who did you miss?"

"The shipping agents. There's only the caretaker in the office now. I spent too long researching on them," Kebble went on disconsolately. His forehead sloped back a little, his jaw almost fell away into his neck, yet gave no impression of weakness. "I thought if I found out the manager's name it would help, but——" His Adam's apple wobbled. "It's Smith."

"Get after him first thing in the morning," Roger said. "We've just had confirmation that the girl was on the S.S. *Kookaburra*, and that her name is Morrison. I've sent Scott to check on Limm. What did *Photography* say?"

"The photo will be ready for the teleprinter by eight-thirty."

"No problems?"

"Old George grumbled about having to treat it as urgent," Kebble said. He was standing straight in front of Roger. "*Is* it so urgent, sir?"

Roger sat back, one hand in his trousers pocket.

"It could be. If it is, we've made a good start and we can really get moving in the morning. If it isn't—no harm's done." He wondered about the missed date with Kitty, what Kitty was like, what the missing Doreen was like. The photograph had been a poor guide, but the enlargement should help. The missing sister worried him, and somehow got under his skin.

"I see," Kebble said. "So that's how you do it?"

Roger only half heard. "Eh?"

"It doesn't matter," Kebble said hurriedly.

Roger forced himself to recall the words, and with a half smile he asked: "So that's how I do what?"

Kebble flushed, and it made him look more than ever like a gobbler.

"I don't want to seem impertinent, sir."

"Did you mean to be?"

"Of course not."

"Then let's have it."

Kebble gave a rather high-pitched laugh.

"You're something of a legend to us younger men, Superintendent. Always pulling off the impossible. If you get moving as quickly as you have over this it means you've a yard start on anyone else—it's like perpetual motion. That's all I meant, sir."

"That's enough butter," Roger said, not ill-pleased. "Detection is like genius, the infinite capacity for taking pains. It couldn't be simpler." After a brief pause, he went on: "Telephone London Airport and find out if a Perce or Percival Sheldon was on Flight 107 for Australia, will you?"

Sheldon was a tall man, in his fifties, running to fat. His luggage was on board the aircraft except for a brief-case and a raincoat, which he carried. He looked hot, and his forehead was beaded with perspiration. His collar was a little too large for him, and the knot of his tie was askew. He stepped out of the telephone booth, jammed his paunch against the handle, then eased himself free; he was too used to such inconveniences to take any notice.

The disembodied voice came over the loudspeaker.

"This is the last call for passengers for Flight 107. Will Mrs. Georgina Thomas and Mr. Percival Sheldon please report at the gangway immediately."

A little woman with a mass of artificial flowers for a hat began to scamper across the lounge, big shiny handbag banging against her knees, umbrella poking out from beneath her arm, a look of dismay on her face. Sheldon thought: "That's Georgina Thomas. I wonder how far she's going." He quickened his pace, something he never liked doing because he became out of breath so easily. He saw a man reading the *Globe,* and on the page turned towards him was the photograph of Denise Morrison.

"Hope she's all right." He had a habit of talking to himself. "Hope I did the right thing. I——"

He broke off, missed his step and went staggering forward.

He was so out of control that he banged bodily into a young girl, and sent her flying, too. A youth by her side cried:

"What the hell do you think you're doing?"

Sheldon didn't hear. He was pitching forward on to the thick red carpet. Pain shot through his chest as if a knife had been driven between his ribs. The pain was so great he could not cry out, he could not breathe, he could do nothing but let his flabby body go where it would.

"Careful!" a man called out.

"He's sick," a woman said in a clear American accent.

"Mind away there!"

Sheldon finally lost his balance. As he fell, his right arm flopped against an upright ash-tray, sending it clattering, and cigarette butts and ash flying. He hit the floor with a heavy thump, quivered, and lay still. His lips were parted and he was breathing through them—just breathing. His eyes were half closed, glazed, lifeless.

"Get a doctor," a man called urgently.

"Doctor?"

"Fetch a doctor."

"*Doctor!*"

An official of the airport came up, with the positive manner of a person who was determined to stop all this fuss. A thickset man among the gathering crowd moved forward and announced:

"I'm a doctor."

They were the last words heard by dying Perce Sheldon. They seemed to bring a crystal clear message of hope, but as the doctor bent over him another spasm of agonizing pain seemed to split his chest in two, his head in two, finally cleaved his whole body.

3

ALARM

ROGER turned over the page of a preliminary report on the Denise Morrison case, already half wishing that he had not decided to stay late. There had seemed so much to do, but most of it would have to wait until morning; nothing yet justified summoning the shipping company manager back to his office. Kebble was waiting for the airport call to come through. Roger ran a finger down the list of people who had 'identified' the girl. It was odd that no one who really knew her had got in touch with the police until late afternoon—the *Globe* was a morning paper. It was odd, too, that no one else had recognized her; girls from Australia weren't rarities here, usually they were quick to meet and make friends with others from their home country. There were private hotels and boarding-houses kept by Australians whose boarders came almost exclusively from down under. It was difficult to believe that the girl had made no friends in London. In any case, there was the sister.

Kebble's telephone bell rang. He picked it up quickly but without fuss.

"Kebble.... Yes, at once, please.... Yes." There was a pause. Roger did not look up, but was intent on the younger officer. "I want to make an inquiry about a passenger flight.... Yes, it is an official inquiry.... Flight 107, for Australia.... Yes. Will you tell me whether a Mr. Perce Sheldon was among the passengers?"

So far it was all calm, competent, done without fuss, and with the manner of a man who knew exactly what he wanted and how to do it. Next moment his voice changed so ludicrously that Roger actually jumped.

"*What?*"

Kebble looked as if he was being told that the plane had crashed, he was so appalled.

"*Are you sure?*"

There was another pause, before he said in a more normal voice:

"Dead for how long?"

Roger sprang up from his chair.

"I see," Kebble said. "Put me on to the Airport Police Office, please. I'll hold on." He covered the mouthpiece with his free hand. "Sheldon died at the airport." He still sounded shocked.

"How?"

"The operator says he just dropped dead."

Roger could not stop himself from exclaiming: "*Dropped dead?*"

"Incredible, isn't it."

Roger didn't speak.

"Must be a coincidence," went on Kebble.

"Could be," Roger conceded, doubtfully. "When the police come on, ask for Inspector Sandys."

"Will you talk to him?"

"Just get the details and tell him you and I are on the way to see him. Oh—find out if the body's been moved. If it hasn't, ask him to keep it there."

"That'll cause a stink at——" Kebble began, then raised the mouthpiece. "Hallo? ... I'm Detective Sergeant Kebble speaking for Superintendent West of Scotland Yard.... Is Inspector Sandys there, please? ... Please."

Roger was looking through the contents of his bag, which was always ready for an emergency. Everything was there—if he used any of the contents on one job he always made a reminder note to make sure he didn't go off without it. He tucked the magnifying glass into its place, closed the box, and turned round.

Kebble was saying: "... should be there in forty minutes." He rang off. "The body's at the Airport Hospital."

"Should have expected that," Roger said. "What did Sandys have to say? All het up at the suggestion of foul play, I suppose."

"He—er—did give me that impression," Kebble admitted. He stood up as Roger rounded the desk.

"We'll take my car," Roger said. "Go and bring it round to the foot of the steps. I'm going to put some steam into *Photography*."

He was out of the room ahead of Kebble, and hurried to the lift with that brisk, thrusting manner which characterized him; a kind of disciplined haste which had become second nature; 'perpetual motion', Kebble had said, and the recollection amused him. There wasn't much to be amused at in this case, and it seemed as if his premonition of trouble had been justified. He wondered whether the years of experience did give a Yard man a kind of prescience.

The lift was at this floor. Roger went up two, then hurried along to *Photography*. This was not the most spacious department at the Yard, but it remained one of the most vital.

Superintendent George Cole, a pale-faced, flabby man with a big double chin, was at a big drawing-desk, where a dozen wet prints were pinned out. He turned his head as Roger entered.

"Gaw," he complained. "I might've known it. Eight-thirty I said and I meant har-past eight."

"George," said Roger, "it's urgent."

"Never had a job of yours that wasn't, in your opinion."

"Nice-looking girl, George, wasn't she?"

"That won't cut any ice. London's full of nice-looking girls and half of them come from Australia, if you can judge from Australia House."

"She came over on the S.S. *Kookaburra*."

"Nice little birdie," said George; that was his brand of humour.

"One of the other passengers on the *Kookaburra* dropped

dead at London Airport half an hour or so ago," Roger declared.

Cole actually gasped, moistened his lips, and ejaculated:
"Gaw. Which one?"

"The man on the right of that snapshot. How soon can we get all of those enlargements round to the Divisions?"

"Smell 'em out, don't you?" Cole said. "Perishing marvel, you are. I'll see it's out by har-past seven."

"George, you're a far better man than they say you are." Roger slapped the plump back, threw: "Thanks," over his shoulder, and hurried out.

Kebble was downstairs, by Roger's black Rover.

"You drive," Roger said.

Rush hour was over, so the Embankment wasn't busy. Kebble knew his London. He weaved and swerved until he reached the flyover beyond Knightsbridge, then put on speed. No one had cause to complain. They reached the main airport gates in thirty-one minutes and were pulling up outside the Airport Police office in thirty-five. As Roger got out, a man at a window on the first floor looked out, and waved.

"I'll come down," he called.

Half a minute later, Roger was saying:

"Sergeant Kebble, Chief Inspector Sandys. Sandy, I'll bet you haven't checked a thing."

"That's where you're wrong," retorted Sandys, with gloomy satisfaction. He was a comparatively short man with a brick-red face, gingery hair going grey, brown eyes, bushy eyebrows, and a mass of freckles on face and hands. "I've checked what time he arrived, where he went, who he talked to, what he ate—but it's all a flicking waste of time. Poor basket had a heart attack."

"Who said so?"

"*I* say so."

"Doctor confirmed it?"

"It's only a matter of time," Sandys insisted.

"It will save us a lot of trouble if you're right," Roger said. "Where's the doctor now?"

"He's still with the corpse," Sandys answered. "Wonder is you didn't bring your tame pathologist along with you as you're in such an almighty hurry."

"Now would I do that until we had a medical opinion?" asked Roger. They were walking towards the main airport building, past the customs bays, up the escalator. "Did Sheldon speak to many people?"

"News-stand, snack-bar waitress, and one official. He'd got his main baggage on board."

"Did he have anyone to see him off?"

"Not at the airport *or* the terminal."

"How did he get here?"

"Airways bus." Sandys took even greater satisfaction in having the answers off pat.

"Do you know if he spoke to any of the other passengers?"

"Couldn't ask 'em," said Sandys. "The plane took off on time without him. Could talk to the pilot by radio if you think it's that important."

"I think it might be," Roger said. "Half an hour won't make any difference, though."

"Don't tell me you're slowing down!" The prospect seemed to delight Sandys as he led the way up a flight of stairs and pointed to a spot which had been roped off—an area perhaps fifteen feet by twenty. "That's where he fell," Sandys declared with even greater satisfaction.

"You must have had second sight," Roger said.

"Just my natural thoroughness," Sandys boasted. For the first time since they had met it seemed to Kebble that he wasn't trying to take a rise out of the Superintendent. "Never do like these sudden deaths, Handsome. Ten per cent chance there's something queer, I always say."

They reached the section which had been roped off with white cords supported by knee-high stands, used for keeping gangways separate; there was nothing sensational about it,

nothing to attract attention. Only a young couple, looking
diffident, were staring at it.

Sandys began to explain what had happened. The young
couple seemed to take a deep interest. Kebble was tempted to
move them on, but Roger West seemed oblivious.

". . . he just toppled over," Sandys said. "Down he went,
out like a light."

The diffident young man, who had a receding chin and a
weak mouth, a chicken to Kebble's turkey, said: "Excuse
me."

Sandys stared at him, his expression enough to frighten off
even a youth who was not timid.

"This is official business."

"I—er—yes, I can see that, but——"

"Cyril, it's not worth wasting any more time," the girl
interrupted. She was shorter than her skinny and meek-looking
companion, stocky, dark-haired, with a fringe which made her
round face slightly like that of a Japanese doll. "Come on."

"No, Sal, I can't."

"Cyril, *please*."

"If you can help us at all we'll be most grateful," Roger
said. "Did you see the incident?"

"Incident!" snorted the girl. "We saw the man die."

"You're quite right, it was much more than an incident."
Roger looked at her gravely. "Did you see what happened
before Mr. Sheldon died?"

The girl didn't answer.

"Yes," declared the weak-looking Cyril. "We did. And he
didn't suddenly fall—he staggered at least twenty feet before
he fell. He banged into my fiancée, that's why we took such
notice of it. But the thing is——"

Sandys looked as if he could wish the young man a thousand
miles away. Kebble was fascinated by the difference between
his manner and that of West.

"Cyril, it might have been nothing. Please don't start a lot
of rumours."

"Is this something you saw or something you heard?" Roger asked the youth.

"Something we saw."

"Both of you?"

"I'm not really sure," the girl said.

"Sal, you know as well as I do that you saw what happened. You are the police, aren't you?" he asked Roger.

"Yes." Roger slipped a card out of his breast pocket and showed it. "This is Inspector Sandys of the Airport Police, and my assistant, Detective Sergeant Kebble. May I have your names?"

"I'm Cyril Gee," the meek-looking young man introduced himself. "My fiancée's Sarah Welling."

"You both have my assurance that anything you say you saw will be treated in confidence," Roger said. "What was it, Mr. Gee?"

"As a matter of fact, it was at the snack bar," answered Gee, quite positively. "The—er—the man who died had some fruit salad and ice-cream, and a cup of coffee. He was reading the newspaper, and suddenly saw something which interested him. A man who had been standing near by came up and jabbed something into him. I'm positive. He stood very close to the man who died, and banged against him. His hand was in his pocket but I saw a pin or a needle or something stick out of the pocket. The man who was eating ice-cream jumped and rubbed his 'rump', but the other chap went off."

Sandys exclaimed: "Good God."

Kebble felt a rush of excitement.

Roger looked straight at Sarah Welling, and asked: "Did you also see that action, Miss Welling?"

"Yes," she said miserably. "It happened all right. The awful thing——"

She broke off.

"The awful thing," said meek-mannered Cyril Gee, "is that we didn't say anything about it to the fat man. We couldn't make up our minds what to do, it was such a surprising thing to happen. The man who used the needle or pin was gone so quickly. He was rather short and was soon lost in the crowd. And the dead man—Sheldon, did you say?"

"Yes."

"Well, he gobbled down the rest of the ice-cream and dashed off," went on Gee. "Sal and I talked about it for a few minutes. We didn't know what to do."

"The truth is, we dithered," the girl put in bitterly.

"Who wouldn't?" asked Roger, with brisk reassurance. "Would you recognize this little man again?"

"Oh yes," asserted Gee.

"Yes," answered Sarah Welling as firmly.

"Sandy," Roger said to the Airport man, "if there was a jab there'll be a puncture—which side, Mr. Gee?"

"Right," answered Gee.

"Thanks. See the doctor, Sandy, will you?"

"Right away." Sandys hurried off.

"Mr. Gee, your information might be invaluable," Roger said. "We've no positive reason to think that Mr. Sheldon died from anything but natural causes, but in a case like this anything which seems inexplicable has to be examined closely. Will you fill in any details you can, and Detective Sergeant Kebble here will make notes. Are you in any great hurry?"

"We only came for a meal and to watch the aircraft take off," Gee said. "We're not in any hurry at all, are we, Sal?"

"I suppose not," the girl agreed resignedly.

"Find a quiet corner, have a drink on Scotland Yard, and tell Sergeant Kebble all you can," Roger said. "I'll see you again before you go."

He nodded, and went off. Not far away in the now busy lounge were some telephone booths. He went into the nearest empty one, and dialled Whitehall 1212.

"Scotland Yard. Can I help you?"

"Give me the Information Room," Roger said.

His voice seemed to put life into the operator.

"At once, sir!" That proved longer than Roger liked and he

turned round. Watching Kebble and the young couple he saw a short man who seemed very interested in them, and wondered if by chance Sheldon had been in this very box.

"Mr. West?" *Information* came at last.

"Get in touch with the City Police, and tell them we need the full passenger list with British addresses, of a ship called the S.S. *Kookaburra* which reached Southampton from Australia about four weeks ago," Roger said. "Better have the officers, too. We need the information tonight. It's the Blue Flag line, and the office is in Throgmorton Street. The manager's name is Smith."

"I've got all that," the *Information* man said. "Where shall I call you?"

"I'll be in soon," Roger said. "Don't let anyone stall you. Two passengers from that ship are dead, one certainly and one possibly of violence. I'd hate anything to happen to the others."

As he put down the receiver he suffered a moment of acute anxiety, almost alarm: for how did he know other passengers weren't dead already?

"Nonsense!" he said aloud, and pushed his way out of the telephone booth, angry with himself but with the shadows as of premonition hovering over him, and the face of the dead girl's sister clear in his mind's eye.

Doreen Morrison was still asleep, but she was breathing more loudly. Now and again she stirred; a movement shifted sheet and blanket and revealed one pale shoulder in the north light of the shabby room.

After a while, her eyes flickered, and opened, and stayed open as she stared blankly at the dingy ceiling.

4

PATHOLOGIST'S REPORT

No shadows were dispersed when Roger stepped into the small room at the airport hospital—really an elaborate first-aid post —where Perce Sheldon's body lay. The body was on a high bed, covered from head to foot with a white sheet, big, bulky, a carcase of hopes and plans, and perhaps deep grief for someone who was half the world away.

On one side of the bed stood Sandys; on the other, a youthful, dark-haired man whose hair grew far back from a pale, shiny forehead. He had big eyes and a button nose, and had something of the look of a golliwog. Roger had met him two or three times, and knew him well enough to respect him both as a doctor and as a man of intelligence.

Sandys glanced round.

"About time," he said gruffly.

"Hallo, Dr. Mason," Roger said.

"Good evening, Mr. West." Mason, on the nearer side to Roger, moved a step and shook hands. "I've just made myself very unpopular with Inspector Sandys."

Roger's smile was set.

"Not natural causes?"

"Possibly not natural causes. The indications were an acute seizure, probably a coronary. Nothing a superficial examination can reveal suggests it. There is a small puncture in the right buttock but it is not conclusively a hypodermic needle puncture."

"Are you able to suggest what caused death?"

"Not until after the autopsy. Do you want me to arrange that?"

Roger said quietly: "Do you want to do it?"

"Not one little bit."

"Then I'll get Whales to do it," Roger said. Dr. Frederick Whales was the pathologist who had carried out the *post mortem* on Denise Morrison. "All right with you, Sandy?"

"I'll have to get approval," Sandys said. "But it'll be okay. When do you want him?"

"As early as possible."

"If I'm fixing that I can't give anything else priority."

"What I'd like you to do as soon as practicable is find which officials were in the waiting-room at the same time as Sheldon. I'll have to use the newspapers for the general public."

Roger's thoughts were running ahead of him. There was so much to do, and telling himself that everything got done eventually did not stop him from fretting because he could not do a dozen things at once. The country editions of the morning newspapers were already being printed but there was time to catch later editions. A request for more eyewitnesses who had seen Sheldon stagger and fall might do more harm than good. If these two deaths had been by the same hand, then the killer would be warned that the police were close on his heels.

"Better wait until I'm sure," Roger said to himself. He went across to a quiet corner where young Cyril Gee, Sarah Welling, and Kebble were standing and talking. There were two glasses on a nearby table.

"How's it going?" asked Roger.

"I've a comprehensive statement signed by both Miss Welling and Mr. Gee," Kebble said. "They've given me their business as well as their home addresses. I think they have done all they possibly can tonight."

Roger said: "Then we needn't keep you a moment longer." He shook hands. "Very many thanks—and we won't worry you again unless we have to."

"You'll have to, I'll bet," Sarah said. She looked tired and unhappy.

"Come on, Sal," Cyril Gee took her arm and led her away.

"He may look a nit but he's no fool," Kebble said, almost to himself. "How are we doing, sir?"

"The local medic has doubts about the cause of Sheldon's death, and Sandys is beginning to hate the sight of me." Roger forced a smile. "I'm going back to the Yard. You stay with Sandys. We want the most comprehensive picture we can of Sheldon's collapse. Humour Sandys, though."

"It would need an angel to do that," said Kebble. "I won't upset him, sir. I'll report as soon as I've got the picture."

Roger nodded, and went across to the police office. For a second time Sandys stopped him with a wave from the window. Soon, the airport policeman came hurrying out.

"Where d'you want the corpse?"

"Cannon Row," Roger answered. "I'll warn 'em it's on the way. Thanks, Sandy. Do me another favour, will you?"

"Can't think why I should, but I will if I can."

"Go easy on young Kebble. He's new to the Yard."

"Young pup," growled Sandys. But he grinned.

Roger got into his car, drove through the tunnel to the main exit, and once on the open road, switched on his radio telephone. *Information* answered almost at once. Roger gave specific instructions for Cannon Row Police Station to prepare for Sheldon in their morgue, and went on:

"Check with City Police about the passenger list. Ask Dr. Whales, if he has his *post mortem* report on Denise Morrison ready, and also ask him to carry out the autopsy on Sheldon first thing in the morning."

Finished, he tried to put the case out of his mind for half an hour. It was a fine starlit evening, there was comparatively little traffic. The glow over central London was so bright that it tinged the night sky with a rainbow of pastel colours. Two youths in an open M.G. which roared past him reminded him of his two sons. He glanced at the dashboard clock. It was nearly eight-fifteen: there should be time to pop into his home, have a snack, enjoy half an hour with Janet, his wife, and the boys. He did not even need to make a detour; the quickest way to the Yard was past the end of Bell Street, where he lived. The temptation was very strong.

His radio crackled. He picked the receiver up.

"West."

"Information here, sir. I've just had a message from Dr. Whales. He'll be in your office in twenty minutes."

"Tell him I'll be there in good time," Roger said. "Any other messages?"

"None, sir."

"Thanks." Roger rang off.

Now he had another preoccupation; why should the pathologist be coming to see him? That wasn't usual, as late in the day as this, unless it was urgent. Thought of going home vanished from his mind. It wasn't until he was walking along to his office, feeling ravenously hungry, that he remembered what he had half planned to do. The office was in darkness. He switched on the light, rang for a messenger, and asked as soon as one came in:

"Get me sandwiches and coffee, will you—quick as you can."

"Right away, sir," the elderly messenger promised.

Roger sat at his desk. Several reports had come in about other cases, and there were twenty-seven more reports about the girl on the photograph; someone had put a note of that number on top of the pile. He thumbed through it quickly, anxiously, and in his heart he hoped for one from Doreen Morrison.

None was there.

There was nothing from anyone who knew her as Denise Morrison, either, so it was a reasonable bet that none of these reports was really about the dead girl. He made sure no one had known her as Brown, the name she had used at the boarding-house then closed the file.

He heard footsteps in the passage, and in spite of his mood, he grinned. No one could ever mistake Dr. Frederick Whales's footsteps. He plonked each foot down, rather as if he were a big fish learning to walk. He was a big heavy man, too, and his waddle of a walk was due entirely to his flat feet.

The door was ajar.

"Hallo, Handsome," Whales greeted him. He looked pale and tired, and also looked as if he had slept in his clothes; he was notorious for his untidiness. "Glad you aren't comfortably settled in the bosom of your family." He sat in the larger of two armchairs. "How about a whisky and soda?"

"When you've told me what this is all about," Roger said.

"One of these days when you want a job done in a hurry I'll refuse," Whales said, as Roger bent down by the side of his desk, opened a cupboard and took out whisky, soda-water, and two glasses. "She wasn't strangled."

Roger's fingers tightened on the neck of the whisky bottle.

"That is to say she didn't die of strangulation," Whales went on. "Someone exerted a lot of pressure on her neck after death. Don't ask me why. The fact remains that she was poisoned. Don't ask me whether the poison was self-administered or not. I don't know."

Roger began to pour out the whisky.

"What killed her?" he asked.

"Digitalis."

"Induced heart failure?"

"Yes."

"How was the digitalis administered?"

"By injection, I presume."

Roger squirted soda-water into the glass which had more whisky and handed it to the doctor.

"Can't you be sure?"

"Good luck." Whales drank as if he were parched. "*Ahhhh!* Be sure of what?"

"How the poison was administered."

"Not absolutely. Injection is the most likely. Have known it taken orally."

"Any in the stomach?"

"No."

"Isn't that conclusive?"

"No," Whales said, "and you know it. It can be absorbed and all traces lost. But there's no doubt about the cause—no doubt at all. Want all the clinical details?" He finished his drink.

"No. Have the other half," Roger said.

"Don't mind if I do, but what are you after?"

"A quick job on another possible victim of poisoning by digitalis."

Whales exclaimed: "Goddamighty." He watched Roger pour out, took the refilled glass, sipped this time and savoured, and then asked: "How quick?"

"Tonight."

"Slave-driver as always." Whales gave a gargantuan yawn and Roger did not think the weariness was wholly assumed. "Where is it?"

"It will be upstairs in the laboratory in half an hour."

"Must go and eat first," Whales said. "I'll be back."

He heaved himself up and padded out.

Roger called Cannon Row, told them to bring Sheldon's body over to the Yard, and had hardly finished when the door opened and the messenger came in with a pile of succulent-looking ham sandwiches and a pot of coffee.

"I didn't think I would disturb you while Dr. Whales was here, sir."

"Quite right," said Roger. "I'd hate to share these." He started on the sandwiches at once, poured out a cup of coffee, and hoped he would be spared ten minutes without interruption. He had seven or eight before the telephone bell rang.

He let it ring for half a minute, while finishing the sandwiches, then picked up the receiver. It might be Kebble, or the City of London Police, Sandys, or young Scott.

"Excuse me," said the operator, "but there's a woman on the line who wants to speak to someone urgently, sir. She sounds in some distress. It's about that photograph in the *Globe*. I know you are handling that."

"What's her name?" asked Roger, almost without thinking.

"She says she's a Miss Doreen Morrison."

Roger felt as if some kind of delayed action shock had caught up with him, and for a moment he could hardly speak. Then he said harshly:

"Put her through, and make sure someone takes a tape recording of the conversation. If I can get an address from her, or a telephone number, I want her traced—*Information* will see to it." He found himself gripping the telephone tightly as the operator said: "Very good, sir." A moment later she went on: "You're through to Superintendent West."

Roger said: "This is Superintendent West. Can I help you, Miss Morrison?"

It seemed an age before she answered, so long that Roger began to wonder if she had gone off the line.

5

TERROR

"ARE you there?" Roger forced himself to be brisk. "Did you hear me?"

After another pause, a girl said huskily: "Yes. Yes, I heard you. Do you—do you know about my sister's photograph?" The words seemed to come reluctantly, as if she were too tired to speak clearly.

Roger could pretend not to know that the photograph had been this girl's 'sister', or he could make her realize he knew a great deal. She could ask questions afterwards.

"Yes, I do," he said. "Where are you?"

She didn't speak.

"Did you hear me?" Roger felt acutely frustrated, and cold with anxiety. There was no way of checking the telephone she was speaking from unless she gave the exchange and number.

She seemed to stifle a yawn. "I don't—I don't know where I am."

It was almost as if she did not know what she was saying, as if her mind or her memory had gone. The vital thing was to find her, and this might be his only chance.

"Miss Morrison, listen very carefully, will you?" Roger said.

There was a sound like a sigh. "Yes."

"Is there a number on the telephone in front of you?"

"A—what?"

"A number."

She paused again, and he had to wait for her. Then she answered, for the first time she seemed to be alert.

"Yes, it's Notting Hill 4785—I *think* the last number is 3, Yes, it's 3. Notting Hill 47853."

"If we get cut off I'll know where to telephone you," Roger spoke quite matter-of-factly, a reassurance in itself. "Are you all right?"

"I—I'm frightened," Doreen Morrison said. "I've been— I've been frightened for so long." There was another pause, before she burst out: "Is Denise all right? *Please* tell me. How did you get her photograph? Is she all right?"

"I'm going to tell you all about it as soon as I can," Roger said. "I don't want to talk much on the telephone. Are you indoors or out of doors?"

"Out of doors," Doreen said. "I got away from——" She broke off, with a little gasp. "Oh, please," she gasped. "Please."

Roger felt quite sure that she wasn't talking to him. For the first time urgency touched with alarm sounded in his voice.

"Doreen! Stay where you are. I will be with you in——"

The line went dead, and stayed dead for perhaps fifteen seconds, before the yard operator spoke in an agitated voice:

"She's gone, sir."

"Did you talk to *Information?*"

"Oh, yes."

"Put me through to——"

"The Inspector in charge is on the line for you, sir." The girl broke off and Robinson's calm voice replaced hers.

"I've two squad and two patrol cars converging on the call-box. We'll pick her up. Don't worry."

"Where was she speaking from?"

"A call-box at the corner of Nash Street, near——"

"I know Nash Street," Roger said. "I'll go straight there."

He rang off, stretched for his hat, and hurried out. A minute later he was at the door of the nearest sergeants' room. Three men in a huddle probably over a smutty joke, all straightened up.

"One of you, take over in my office," Roger said. "Tell the operator to put anyone who calls about Denise Morrison—know whom I'm talking about?"

"Yes, sir—this morning's unknown."

"Right. Have all calls about her put through to you. I'm interested in anyone who knows her as Morrison or Brown, and I want to be able to talk to them tonight. Got that?"

Three big men spoke like eager schoolboys. "Yes, sir."

Roger went hurrying on.

A constable was standing by his car, and opened it as Roger reached it.

"A bit late going home, sir."

"If only I was," Roger almost groaned.

In fact, the thought was little more than a reaction; he wanted only to be at Notting Hill Gate for the next half-hour. If anything had happened to the other sister——

Surely it couldn't.

If Kebble or anyone else said that to him, he would rasp: Don't be a damned fool.

Of course it could.

He could hear the girl saying she was frightened; he could

hear her saying: "Please, oh please," in a tone of horror and in desperate pleading.

"Please," Doreen Morrison said with a catch in her voice. "Please don't take me back to that room."

The man at the door of the telephone kiosk, a small man with thin, dark hair and a thin, pale face and wishy-washy blue eyes, smiled at her. He had a charming smile; it seemed intended to take a load of anxiety off her.

"You will be all right," he assured her. "Don't you want to see your sister again?"

"Yes, yes, but you promised I would see her this afternoon."

"She was delayed," the small man said. He took Doreen's arm, and held it very tightly, tucked under his elbow, so that she had to keep pace with him; if she didn't, it would hurt. She knew, because he had held her like that before.

He hurried along the narrow street—Nash Street, which led off the main road from Bayswater. There were tall, narrow houses all joined together. Many people thronged the streets, most of them black-skinned. N oone took any notice of Doreen or the man. They reached a corner of a street which was even narrower. Here the dim lights at windows and the slightly brighter ones at the street lamps showed the dilapidated houses, front rooms overcrowded with people but with very little furniture.

"Please——" Doreen began.

The man gave her arm a twist. Pain streaked from her wrist to her elbow, shot up to her shoulder.

"*Oh!*"

"Don't talk any more," the man ordered roughly.

A car passed. In it were two men who looked like policemen. They glanced at her. She knew that she appeared to be walking happily arm-in-arm with her companion. He twisted again, and she turned her head away from the police involuntarily, because the pain was so great.

The car was a long way off when she was able to look straight ahead again. Fewer people were here—and fewer houses. This was a deserted area, with few buildings standing after the bombing which had devastated so much of London before she had been born.

One house had two lighted windows and a light at the front door; otherwise it was in darkness. The man propelled her towards it. As she drew nearer she felt panic born of the quiet terror which had been with her for so long. She had been in that house for two weeks, almost a prisoner, believing that she had to stay if she wanted to help Denise.

Suddenly, awfully, she knew that Denise was dead.

In that moment, walking against her will through the semi-darkness of the street, she seemed to see the photograph which had been in the *Daily Globe* more vividly than she had before. Denise was dead; Denise, sleeping, had never looked like that.

They were close to the front door of the house. The small man's grip on her slackened because they were so near. Out of panic and desperation Doreen felt an upsurge of courage. She must not go with this man. Denise was dead, and anything might happen to her.

She pulled herself free.

She pushed the man and kicked him. He went staggering to one side. She began to run, skirt riding up her slim legs, higher, higher, giving her greater freedom of movement. She raced along. Not many months ago she had run in the State Championships at Adelaide, third in the two thousand yards. She felt like the wind. She did not look round, it might lose her precious seconds. She heard no sound of footsteps in pursuit. As she began to gasp for breath, she felt a great sense of elation.

He wasn't chasing her. He——

He appeared in front of her, from a side alley. There was a smear of blood on his forehead. He wasn't smiling; he looked as if he could kill.

"No!" she cried.

She dodged to one side, but he shot out his leg and she tripped. She had not a second to prepare herself, and just crashed down. Surprise and shock were so complete that she did not know even a spasm of fear. She struck her head against the pavement and lost consciousness. She was not even aware that the little man bent down, picked her up, and began to carry her towards the alley which led round the back of the derelict houses.

A police car waited at the corner of Nash Street as Roger drew up. A divisional detective sergeant, a man in his fifties, came up and put his head through the open window.

"Any luck?" Roger demanded.

"Not yet," the sergeant answered casually.

Roger said harshly: "You mean you've lost her."

"Never had her to lose," the divisional man retorted; he was too old a hand to worry too much or be too troubled by a Yard officer in a bad temper.

"Has anyone seen her?" asked Roger.

"Can't be sure," the divisional man replied. "Our chaps and the Flying Squad boys are following several leads. Only a matter of time, Super."

"Time," Roger echoed. He sounded as bitter as he felt, and the divisional man realized something was seriously wrong but did not know what it was. It did not seem to trouble him. Roger opened the door of his car and got out. There was no sense in antagonizing this man, who was simply doing a routine job.

His radio sounded: "Calling Superintendent West. Calling..."

Roger stretched inside and picked up the receiver.

"West speaking."

"Information here," a man said. "Two messages for you, sir. Detective Sergeant Kebble is on his way back from the airport, and will be in your office whatever time you return."

"Yes."

"A Mr. Lancelot Smith is coming to see you in about an hour's time—he will have the list of passengers and officers of the S.S. *Kookaburra* with him. Should have said that was a message from the City chaps, sir."

"Good," said Roger. "Thanks." He put back the receiver, only a little less gloomy. They had lost the girl, and there could be no doubt of danger to her. He turned away from the telephone as a car drew up just behind him. He recognized a sergeant of the Flying Squad, but the puzzling thing was that the man was on his own.

As he got out, obviously in a hurry, he recognized Roger.

"Evening, sir. I think we might know where that girl is."

Roger's heart began to thump.

"Where?"

"I was going along with another sergeant, and saw her and a man who fits the description put out earlier—the man of London Airport, sir. Short, small chap, pale, thin dark hair. Fair girl was with him. They were walking very close together. She didn't look as if she was having fun, though."

"Where's the other sergeant?"

"Keeping track of them. They're in Johnson Street."

"Take me there, will you?" Roger said. He saw the Divisional man's eyes brighten, and suddenly remembered his Christian name. "Charley, spread the word round—and close in on Johnson Street."

"Right away!" Charley looked delighted.

Roger got in with the Flying Squad man, who started off as if he would ram any car which got in his way. He swung round one corner, then another, driving with the effortless ease of the expert.

"Describe the girl," Roger ordered.

"Fair, about five-four, good figure, rather full calves—very general I know, but so was the description."

"Could be the right one," Roger agreed. He was aware of the number of coloured people staring, because the car was moving so fast. They took another corner, missing a cyclist by a foot or so. Roger bit his lip. The Squad man slowed down perceptibly, and by the time they reached the next cross-roads, they seemed to be crawling. A man appeared from the doorway of a house which was in utter darkness.

Roger recognized a sergeant of the Flying Squad, who spoke before anyone had a chance to speak.

"They're in that house across the road."

"Sure?" demanded Roger.

"Positive. Two local uniformed men are at the back, sir."

The house across the road had lights at two ground floor windows; everywhere else was in darkness except the front door, where a dim light shone through frosted glass panels.

"I'm going over," Roger said. "Don't stand on any ceremony if there seems to be any trouble."

The sergeant who had brought him here said hastily: "Let me go, sir."

"Not this time." Roger smiled, and turned in the near-darkness. Nothing would release him from his present tension except action.

The other man was right, this wasn't a job for a senior officer. But he felt a strange sense of personal involvement, an irresistible compulsion to go himself. It was as if he accepted the full responsibility for making sure that Doreen Morrison did not suffer the same fate as her sister.

6

NEEDLE

DOREEN kept on thinking "No, no, no." She had come round halfway up the dark stairs of the house where she had slept that day. The man, Jessup, was half carrying, half dragging her up them. He was breathing very hard, making a whistling sound through his nostrils. His footsteps clumped and slithered on the boards of the stairs. A board creaked loudly. He stopped and let Doreen slide down so that she rested on her feet, leaning against him. Her breasts pushed against his thin chest, but she was oblivious of that, oblivious of the way her skirt had rucked up high above her knees.

The refrain did not stop. "No, no, no."

Yet she was too dazed, too weak, to think or to struggle. She heard sounds and was aware of movement. Then a loud creak made her realize that the door of her room had opened.

She gasped: "No!"

She made a tremendous effort, and thrust herself backwards, away from him. On that instant she heard him swear, viciously, obscenely. Their bodies were no longer touching, but suddenly she felt his hands at her neck. With furious strength he gripped her. The breath seemed to be locked in her lungs, suddenly there was hard, frightening pressure round them. Hands still clutching, Jessup held her at arms' length and pushed her backwards. Her legs almost doubled up. She would have fallen but for that terrible pressure on her neck. Her chest was heaving as she tried to draw in breath, but his hold was too tight, the pressure on her lungs seemed to crush her.

He flung her away from him.

The back of her legs caught against the edge of the divan bed. She toppled back, and fell heavily, but she could *breathe*. Air forced itself into her lungs, the pain of relief from pressure was almost as great as the pain from the pressure itself. She was past thinking, almost past caring, because the precious air was hers again, and the steel-like band across her chest had broken.

Light went on, she was aware of it.

Jessup moved, and she knew that too, but did not know where he went or what he did. The light was bright against her eyes, and all she wanted was to lie there, eyes shut tightly, the breath of life creeping into her.

There were shadowy movements; Jessup's.

There were tiny, metallic sounds, as well as the sound of his laboured breathing.

Doreen did not know that he was preparing a hypodermic syringe, filling it from the ampoule which quivered in his right hand. Breathlessness, fear, perhaps even a kind of hatred for himself made his whole body quiver. There was a sucking sound as the deadly liquid filled the glass body of the syringe.

Her eyes flickered open.

In a moment of terrible clarity she realized what he was about to do. Her skirt was rucked up to her waist, inches of her thigh were bare. He held the hypodermic syringe in his right hand. She gave a convulsive leap but he anticipated it. He thrust his left hand down with crushing weight on to her breast, forcing her against the bed, and raised his right leg and bent it and knelt on her legs right on the knee caps. She was now so petrified that all she could hear was the thumping of her heart. She saw Jessup's face contorted as if in rage, saw his lips move as if in speech. She made a desperate but hopeless effort to shift to one side, but could not.

The hall of the house was empty when Roger stepped into it. Faint sounds of music came from a room on the right, the door of which was open. The other door, on the left, was closed, but light shone beneath it and at one side.

He heard footsteps on bare boards, and stood for a few seconds, straining his ears. Undoubtedly they were on the stairs, some way up. The music seemed to grow louder, and to drown them. He started to climb, peering upwards all the time. The only light came from a tiny bulb at a landing almost straight above his head. Beyond it there were vague, moving shadows. He went up quickly, keeping to one side, for stairs did not squeak so loudly close to the wall. He was halfway up when he heard a loud creak above him—a long way above. That was followed by more footsteps, a rumble of sound as if someone was staggering.

He thought he heard a gasp, perhaps a stifled scream.

He raced up the stairs, as a door slammed. The light was on this landing, and he saw nothing beyond but darkness. He sped up the next flight of stairs to a second landing, and as he reached it light framed a door above his head.

The light had just been switched on.

He went towards it with controlled speed, making hardly a sound. The music had. faded, all he could hear were movements beyond the door now framed with light. He could rush at it, or approach with stealth. Was the girl in acute danger at this moment? He told himself that he could not even be positive that Doreen Morrison was there. If Kebble or any junior acted on impulse, as he was doing, he would slap them down hard when he heard of it.

He reached the landing and the door.

He had to be sure Doreen was inside. He might hear a word or two of vital importance if he listened, too. He pressed his ear close to the door, every nerve strained to catch any sound.

He thought someone was gasping for breath. There was another noise, a muffled voice, a creaking of springs. He could thrust open this door and disturb two people in the privacy of their deep passions; drunk or sober they had every right. . . .

He had to take the chance, so he turned the handle, and pushed; the door opened a few inches, without creaking. In the bright light of a single lamp he saw a man kneeling on a girl, whose legs alone showed, whose head and body were hidden. The man's right arm was held high and the light glinted on a hypodermic syringe and its needle.

"*I didn't want to kill you,*" the man was saying in a gasping way.

Roger said in a taut voice: "You're not going to."

He thrust the door wide open as the man spun round. For a moment the girl's head and shoulders appeared. She looked as pale as death and her eyes were closed. Her skirt was rucked up about her waist, her right stocking was a mass of ladders.

The man did not speak, just stood there with the syringe still in his right hand. He was almost as pale as the girl, and his pallor made his eyes look black as beads. He was short, weak-looking, and his hair grew far back from his forehead.

Roger went a step nearer, his mouth very dry.

"Drop that syringe," he ordered. "I am a detective officer, and——"

"Get away," the little man said in a choky voice.

"Drop it, and don't waste time." Roger took a step nearer, but was very wary. This man was desperate; that showed in his eyes and in the tension of his body. "Do as you're told."

He began to move forward again.

The little man took a step towards him, the syringe held forward in his right hand, like a dagger. His thumb was on the plunger. If he got too close he could jab that needle in.

How much was a fatal dose?

"Drop it!" Roger barked.

The man leapt at him, needle thrusting at his face. As it came it seemed to become enormous, looming as deadly as a rapier. In that split second Roger felt wild panic. If he swept the arm aside the needle might jab into his arm or his hand.

It was like a blinding light.

He dropped to his knees. The man's sleeve brushed the top of his head but there was no sharp pain. He brought his head up with all the force he could, into the man's groin, and heard the agonized, hissing intake of breath as the man staggered back. The syringe dropped close to Roger's knees. He got up, hardly breathing, staring at the man, who had banged into a chair and was now doubled up in anguish. Roger raised his right foot. The impulse to stamp on the syringe was almost overwhelming. He brought his foot down, but at the last second snatched it away. A little liquid had oozed out of the needle and made a tiny blob on the shiny linoleum.

The other man straightened up, made a futile effort to attack again, and was caught with a spasm of pain. Roger forced himself to act, stepped past him, caught his right wrist, and thrust his arm up behind him in a hammer-lock. He didn't say a word as he stared at the girl.

She still lay on her back, staring at him, as if she was petrified.

"It's all right," Roger said gently. "You needn't worry any more."

Her lips were parted, her eyes wide open, velvety eyes but vacant now.

"You're going to be all right," Roger assured her. "I'll be back in——"

He broke off, tensing up for a moment. There was a sound at the door, and no way of being sure that the man hadn't an accomplice. Then the big form of the Flying Squad man blocked the doorway.

"You okay, sir?" he was anxious.

"Yes." Roger could hardly hear his own voice, it was so hoarse. "Take this chap, charge him with attempting to cause grievous bodily harm, and have him sent to the Yard at once."

"Right!" The Flying Squad man seemed glad of the chance. Then he caught sight of the girl, and gaped.

"Tell Charley to send a doctor here," Roger said. "Shock case, mostly." As the other moved forward, his voice sharpened. "Mind that needle!" The man's big foot was only inches away from the syringe. He evaded it, and took a grip on the little man's arm.

Roger was staring at the girl, and the Flying Squad man hadn't got a good grip. The prisoner wrenched himself free and hurtled towards the door. The sergeant shot out a foot, and the man ran into it and pitched forward. The sergeant moved very quickly for a big man, bent down, and yanked him to his feet by the scruff of his neck.

"I'll watch him, sir."

Roger nodded. He turned back to the girl, but she hadn't moved, and was staring in that vacant way just as she had before. Her skirt was still rucked up. She had full, firm thighs, and he noticed her rather big but well-shaped calves. She wore a frilly white blouse which looked grubby.

Roger drew closer. There was no blemish on the girl's legs

or on her cheeks, just the pallor of someone who had been ill, and kept indoors for a long time. He pulled up a chair and sat close to her taking her hand and feeling for her pulse.

"You've nothing else to worry about," he assured her gently. "You're quite safe now. I'm Superintendent West. You talked to me on the telephone. Do you remember?"

She didn't speak; he could not even be sure that she heard him. Her pulse was slow, her forehead cold.

"You have nothing else to worry about," he assured her again.

He was almost glad that she did not appear to understand, for it was not true. When she recovered, and the effect of this shock had gone, she would be faced with the news of the death of her sister.

"Do you know the name of the man who was with you?" he asked.

It was a formality. He had at least to try to make her answer questions, but there was no hope of an answer.

"You can be absolutely sure you have nothing more to worry about," he repeated with great deliberation. If he could make her understand that it might give her sufficient strength to draw on later.

Two things happened in the next moment, when he was preoccupied only with thought of helping Doreen Morrison. Her eyes widened, as if in sudden fear, and as he thought it was due to sharp recollection of what had happened, he heard a squeak behind him, as of a footstep on the shiny linoleum.

He felt an almost irresistible impulse to jump round, but stayed close to the girl. Her lips began to quiver and there was no doubt of her fear. Another squeak sounded—closer. A gasping sound came from the girl, terror was in her eyes.

Without getting up, Roger swung round, sending the chair flying.

A man was only two or three feet away from him, reaching forward, a knife in his hand held as if to plunge into Roger's back—or into the girl's breast. Roger kept going, arms outstretched, clutching at the man's legs. In that split second he had no time to think, his actions were based on reflexes, not on thought. He saw the man's right foot move, realized what was coming; that the man was going to kick him. He made another desperate effort to clutch the other's foot, then saw the shiny toe of the shoe swinging towards him; it seemed like the foot of a giant. He rolled to one side. The foot scraped along his temple, rasping and painful but with little force.

The girl screamed—a piercing sound of horror.

God!

Roger squirmed round, on the floor. The man was standing over the girl, his right arm raised. Roger could not see the knife but knew it was in that poised right hand ready to sweep down into the girl's body. The foot of the divan was close to Roger, but the man was out of reach. Roger placed both hands on the side of the divan and thrust with all his strength. The divan shifted with startling speed, casters sliding over the smooth floor. The man by it struck his murderous blow, but the knife plunged into the divan, inches from the girl.

The door banged open. A man called:

"Are you all right?"

The man by the bed snatched at the knife, touched but failed to grasp it, then rushed at a police constable who was already halfway across the room. The constable looked small and frail, the would-be murderer big and powerful. He did exactly as he had with Roger: kicked out brutally. His foot caught the policeman in the groin, and as the uniformed man went staggering back, the attacker rushed out of the room. There was a shout, a bang, a thud.

Roger picked himself up, heavily. The policeman banged against a chair, and doubled up. The girl lay absolutely still, staring at the door.

It opened, and a plain-clothes man appeared.

"Did you get him?" asked Roger.

"The man who ran out of here—no, sir. He ducked into another room and out of a window. Are you all right?"

Roger said slowly: "Yes. Go downstairs and have a general call put out for the man. Height about six feet, swarthy-skinned, broad nose, wearing dark clothes, a dark scarf, and a cloth cap. Say where he was last seen. Got all that?"

"Yes, sir." The man hurried out.

Roger went over to the policeman, who was bending down with his knees tightly pressed together. He straightened up, looking very pale.

"Want any help?" Roger asked.

"Often had worse while kicking a football about," the man said ruefully.

Roger went back to the girl. She had not moved, and did not appear to see him. He studied the knife. The handle was covered with cloth, like a bandaged finger, and there would be no prints on it. He pulled it out. The blade was razor sharp and had a needle point.

He could not repress a shudder.

Footsteps sounded on the stairs, and soon a snowy-haired young man appeared, carrying a bag. A squad sergeant was just behind him. The first man was a Divisional Police Surgeon. He came forward with a diffidence which reminded Roger of weak-chinned Cyril Gee, of London Airport.

"Your patient," Roger said, standing up.

The girl gave no sign that she had heard.

Roger went across and began to pick up the syringe, handling it with great care. Soon the Divisional men were here in strength, photographers, fingerprint men, every expert who might help. It would have been superfluous to give instructions; these men knew exactly what was wanted. Roger waited until Doreen Morrison was taken out on a stretcher, and had a word with a Divisional Detective Inspector who came to take charge.

"I'll take the knife over to the Yard," Roger said.

"Let me check it first, will you?" the Divisional man asked. "I'll send it over."

"Suit yourself," Roger agreed.

Two uniformed policemen including the victim of the attack were at the front of the house, where a crowd had gathered, mostly Jamaicans; there were a surprising number of children, whose big, dark eyes reminded Roger of Doreen. Someone had brought his own car up, and one of the policemen pushed his way towards it and opened the door for Roger.

"Thanks." He nodded and drove off. Soon he was out of the narrow streets and in the wide thoroughfares. He turned towards the West End. It was nearly half past nine, he was going to be home very late. He stifled a yawn; bursts of action and bursts of tension took more out of him these days than they had a few years ago. He wasn't so quick, either, he thought sourly, or he would not have let the second attacker get away. Angry with himself, and suffering from reaction, he pulled off the main road near Marble Arch, lit a cigarette, and switched on the car radio. There was a Brahms Concerto, he didn't know its name. He made himself relax for ten minutes, half listening, thinking over all that had happened. Then he jerked himself out of the reverie, and drove to the Yard. The courtyard was almost empty but as he pulled in two Squad cars raced out with their usual fierce urgency.

No one spoke to him on the way to his office. He saw light at the sides, and heard voices. Kebble and who? The shipping agency manager, Smith, of course. He whistled a tune to announce his arrival. When he opened the door, Kebble was heading for it.

"Hallo, sir."

"Hallo, Sergeant."

"I've just been talking to Division about what happened."

"Been quite a night, hasn't it?" Roger said.

A man was rising from the armchair. Sitting, he seemed quite normal, but on his feet he was very short—almost a dwarf. He had rather big, coarse features, heavy-lidded eyes, big hands.

"This is Mr. Lancelot Smith, sir."

"I am pleased to meet you." Smith had a deep, rasping

voice. "And very distressed indeed to hear about the death of two people who were passengers on the S.S. *Kookaburra*. I have with me the list of passengers." His accent was very slightly foreign and his enunciation too precise. He handed Roger a printed list, and then added: "Also a list of the ship's officers." He handed this over, and Roger saw a passport-size photograph against each name. "Also of the crew, if that is of assistance."

Roger took the lists, glancing almost casually at the photographs until he saw one which made him forget everything else.

The man he had stopped from killing Doreen Morrison was here, Third Officer Thomas Jessup of the S.S. *Kookaburra*.

7

DEATH AFAR OFF

LANCELOT SMITH obviously realized that there was trouble. Kebble, in the background, moved forward to look at the photographs. Roger put his forefinger on Jessup, and asked:

"How well do you know the crew?"

"In person, hardly at all except the Captain, Chief Officer and Chief Engineer. Otherwise I know their history and record. This was the Third Officer. Do you know him?"

"Yes, slightly. You said 'was'."

"He left the ship in London."

"Wasn't he signed on for a round trip?"

"He was unsatisfactory," Smith declared.

"In what way?"

"Superintendent, such matters are confidential."

"We are investigating a murder."

Smith moistened his thick lips.

"I wish to assist in every way I can, of course. This would be in confidence, would it not?"

"Yes."

"There were thefts on board the ship, mostly from the crew and officers, some from the passengers. Jessup was asked to leave the ship."

"Did you accuse him of theft?"

"There is no doubt he knew why he was not wanted."

"What would you expect him to do?"

Smith shrugged. "Get another ship, no doubt."

"So that he could repeat his thefts there?"

Smith said slowly: "Nothing was proved, Superintendent. You cannot ruin a man because of suspicion."

"Who else knew of these suspicions?"

"The Captain, Chief Officer, and Chief Engineer knew officially." Smith raised a big, ungainly hand. "Why are you so interested in this man?"

"He is under a charge of attempting to cause bodily harm to another of the *Kookaburra*'s passengers," Roger answered flatly.

"Another?" Smith sounded shocked.

"And he will probably be charged with committing one of the murders," Roger went on. "I want all available information about him as early as possible, Mr. Smith. Everything."

"I shall cable for further details tonight," Smith promised. He looked scared now, and very ugly; almost cretinous.

"Did he have access to poisons?" Roger asked.

"*Poisons?*"

It would be easy to lose one's temper with this man.

"Presumably the *Kookaburra* carried medical supplies."

Smith took out a handkerchief and dabbed the back of his thick neck.

"That is so," he admitted. "Had Jessup——" He moistened his lips.

"Yes?"

"Jessup was our first-aid officer, in charge of supplies of the Sick Bay. You think he stole poisons——" Smith's voice trailed off.

"It's certainly possible," said Roger. "Do you know if any digitalis was carried on board?"

"I—I cannot be sure. I will find out from Sydney, as quickly as I can."

"Where is the *Kookaburra* now?"

"She is four days out of Hong Kong, heading for Sydney."

"How long will the voyage take?"

"Usually it would take twelve days."

"Are the rest of the officers the same as on the outward voyage?"

"Yes, Superintendent."

"What about the crew?"

"It is mostly a Chinese crew, and there were few changes. These I can check for you in the morning." Smith backed to his chair and sat down, dabbing at his forehead.

"Do you know if a man answering this description was among the crew?" Roger repeated the description he had already broadcast to the Divisions. It was vague; his own impression of the man with the cap pulled low over his eyes and the scarf up over his chin *was* vague.

"It might answer a number of people," Smith said reasonably. "But no one I knew on board the *Kookaburra* was like that. No one. You—you said that Jessup attacked *another* passenger?"

"He attacked Doreen Morrison," Roger told him. "Have you the European or United Kingdom addresses of the other passengers on the outward journey?"

"Yes," Smith said. He pointed to the passenger list in Roger's hand. "They are all there. But—but you have caught Jessup, you say." For the first time the shipping man seemed to brighten. "He can do no more harm, then? There is no danger for the other passengers."

"We don't know yet," Roger said. "There's far too much we don't know. Is there any reason why Jessup should want to kill the two Morrison girls, or Mr. Sheldon?"

"I know of none."

"Did they ever accuse him of theft?"

"I do not know."

"Are you sure you don't?"

"Yes, Superintendent." Smith acquired an unexpected dignity as he squared his shoulders. "I am quite sure. However, some of the passengers accused him, that is certain. I do not know who they were. It was a matter for the ship's master, you understand."

"Surely he would log any such charge."

"I did not see his log," Smith said. "Superintendent, I will afford you all the help in my power but I cannot give you information which is not at my disposal."

After a pause, Roger forced a smile.

"No, of course not." He wondered whether he was too much on edge, perhaps suffering from shock reaction, or whether Lancelot Smith's appearance was sufficiently grotesque for him to take a dislike to the man, and so be prejudiced. "You've been very good. I would like the address, telephone number, and cable address of your Sydney office, then we needn't worry you again until the morning."

Smith's eyes positively glistened.

"All the information is on the lists, the Sydney and London postal and cable addresses, all are there. Superintendent, anything I can do is as good as done."

"Thank you," Roger said. "Mr. Smith."

"Yes?"

"Do you know of any reason why anyone should want to kill passengers of your ship?"

"It is a complete mystery to me," Smith declared earnestly. "A complete mystery. Unless perhaps Jessup is not a sane man. A psychopath might be so deeply insulted that he would kill anyone who——" Smith stopped, as if he knew that Roger wasn't impressed, as if he himself was not really impressed by his own arguments. In a whispering voice he insisted: "It is possible. There are such men."

"Perhaps there are," Roger said. "Sergeant, show Mr. Smith the main door, will you?"

Smith did not offer to shake hands, but went out as if he could not get away from Roger quickly enough. The two sets of footsteps sounded along the passage, but soon faded. Roger turned to his desk, rounded it, and sat down. There was something in Smith's manner he didn't like at all. By now he should have thrown off any reaction, should be elated. The girl was alive, and shock symptoms would not last long. One murderer was caught, the other would be picked up soon.

How could he say that with certainty?

All the years of experience warned him against taking anything for granted, but surely Jessup *was* the murderer of Denise Morrison and Sheldon. He had the description from Cyril Gee which tallied, the man himself, the hypodermic syringe in his pocket. He had actually seen Jessup in the act of plunging the needle in. What doubt could there be? He took the syringe out of his pocket and put it on the blotting-pad in front of him. Needle and glass glistened. He heard Kebble's footsteps, and Kebble opened the door and stalked in.

"Take this thing up to the lab. and have the contents analysed," Roger said. "Tell 'em it might be digitalis."

"Right." Kebble leaned across and picked up the blotting-pad.

"Where does young Cyril Gee live?"

"Victoria—just behind the Army and Navy Stores," Kebble answered.

"Know his phone number?"

"Victoria 81345."

Roger grinned. "Thanks." He picked up the telephone and gave the number before Kebble reached the door. "Keb."

Keb turned, balancing the blotting-pad.

"What did you make of Smith?"

"I thought he had a load on his mind," Kebble said grimly. "I had a feeling he knew there was trouble brewing."

Roger nodded, Kebble went out, the telephone bell rang. It was so often, too often, like this; no time really to think, to get a balanced view, to test one's own reactions for mistakes and the facts for fallacies.

"Your Victoria number, sir," the operator said.

"Thanks.... Mr. Gee?" Roger put his reflections aside and made his voice sound affable.

Gee did not.

"I thought you weren't going to bother us——" there was a fractional pause, before he corrected: "bother me again."

"Only in emergency," Roger said. "I'm really sorry. Can you come over to the Yard?"

"What, *now*?"

"Yes, please," Roger said. "I'll gladly send a car for you."

"Oh, all right," Gee said, with ill grace. "I'll be ready in ten minutes." There was a whisper of sound in the background, then Gee hung up across his own rather miserable: "I can't refuse."

Roger was smiling faintly. All his awareness of the way people lived did not save him from a prudish reaction of surprise if there were indications of pre-marital getting together. Did they share a flat? What the hell was it to do with him? He rang off, telephoned the sergeants' room, sent a man to pick up Gee, and then sat back. The Yard was very quiet. He was feeling easier in his mind, the sense of brooding danger was almost gone. If only word would come of the capture of the man who had attacked him and the girl at Notting Hill Gate, he would be himself again.

A man called: "Have you an appointment, sir?"

Hurried footsteps followed, drawing nearer. Roger heard two men approaching, and pushed his chair back. Lancelot Smith appeared, mouth open and breathing very hard; a messenger was behind him, looking questioningly at Roger.

"It's all right," Roger told him. "Yes, Mr. Smith?"

Smith came right in.

"There's something—I ought to—have told you." He gasped for breath after every two or three words, partly from nerves, partly because he had hurried. "I couldn't—bring myself—to."

The man behind him closed the door.

"Very good of you to come back," Roger said, rounding his desk. "Sit down and take your time." He held the man's arm as he sat down. "Would you like a drink?"

"No thank—thank you. I don't—drink alcohol." Smith sat on the edge of his chair, that near-cretinous face twisted in distress. "One of the—one of the other ship's officers died in—in mysterious circumstances in Hong Kong. Four days ago. It was—sudden death, like these people here, but—but—but——"

He could not utter the words.

"Jessup couldn't have killed him, could he?" Roger helped out. All his own fears and anxieties flooded back, but he forced himself to speak dispassionately: "Let me have the full details, please."

He was writing: *First Engineer, Neil Sanderson, native of Townsville, Queensland, aged 24*—when Kebble came in. Kebble showed how startled he was only for a moment, then behaved as if he had expected to find Smith here.

"What time is it in Hong Kong?" Roger asked Kebble, when Smith had gone.

"About five or six hours ahead of us, aren't they?" Kebble said.

"Find out, then see if you can get a senior officer on the telephone. If you can't, cable for details of this engineer's death." Roger was very brisk.

"Right."

"I'll go and see Cyril Gee," Roger said.

He went out, as Kebble picked up the telephone. It was ten o'clock, and he felt as if the night would never end. He plonked his feet down heavily, trying not to hurry too much. Gee was in a waiting-room one floor below. He was standing up, giving an impression of angry impatience. He looked tired; and he looked as weak-willed as a man could.

"I hope this is necessary," he said, more peevish than tart.

"If it weren't I wouldn't have asked you to come," Roger said. "I've arranged for an identification parade across at Cannon Row Police Station—half a minute away. I hope you will see someone whom you recognize."

"You've *got* him?" Gee's voice rose on that instant.

"I've a suspect," Roger said. "Don't speak until we're out of earshot, will you?"

He felt as nearly sure as he could that Gee would pick out Jessup as the man who had jabbed a needle into Sheldon at the airport, but as they entered the room where two policemen and five men in ordinary clothes were waiting, he felt a wave of doubt. The five men were all much the same in appearance, on the small side, and each wore dark clothes and a dark trilby hat. The lighting was simulated daylight, as good as one could get for identification at night.

They passed along the line, where Jessup was in the middle. They passed in front of each man and Gee did not show any sign of recognition; he was over his peevishness, apparently right on top of himself.

They went out.

"It was the man in the middle," Gee stated flatly. "You've got him all right. Congratulations. Sorry I was so bad-tempered."

"Forget it." Roger warmed to him. "I needn't keep you any longer tonight but I may have to call you as a witness later."

Gee grimaced.

"My fiancée told me from the start that I was a mug to get involved in this," he said. "She doesn't go for that guff about the responsibility of the citizen."

"It's a good thing you do, or we might still be looking for this chap, and another girl might have been dead." Roger shook hands very firmly, only half amused by the glow of delight in Gee's eyes; the man wasn't much more than twenty-two or three, only a couple of years or so older than his own boys. He saw Gee to the Yard's gate himself, and saw and heard him driven off. Roger went back to Cannon Row, relieved in one way, anxious and uncertain in another. There was something on his mind, something he'd forgotten. He could not recall it. Jessup hadn't yet uttered a word, and now he had to be questioned. It might take a long, long time. He stifled a yawn, and went into Cannon Row Police Station. First a cup of strong coffee, then——

The night duty Inspector of the police station was walking along the passage towards Roger. There was no doubt that he brought trouble with him. Tall, grey-haired, one of the most experienced and reliable officers on the Force, this was one of the few occasions when Roger had seen his looks give him away.

Roger waited for the blow.

"Jessup's killed himself," the Inspector announced bluntly. "He'd a tablet of cyanide of potassium hidden. He knew he'd be identified, of course, knew he hadn't a chance."

Roger stood absolutely still.

"I'm damned sorry," the Cannon Row man went on. "And I can't blame anyone but myself. I was present when he was searched. How bad does that make things for you?"

After a pause, Roger said bitterly: "God alone knows." Now he had no cause at all for elation, only for a new kind of anxiety. If a man would kill himself rather than be made to talk, what cause did he serve? What hideous secrets had he taken into death?

Roger gripped the other man's forearm.

"Bad luck, Jim." He paused again, and then went on: "I'd better go and see him."

8

MESSAGE FROM HONG KONG

HALF AN HOUR later Roger turned into his office, where the lights blazed. He was still needled by the sense of some unknown but terrible thing, by a desperate anxiety to learn the truth. He wondered when Doreen Morrison would be able to talk—he ought to have inquired how she was. He saw Kebble at his desk, looking young and very wide awake. Kebble grinned and put a finger to his lips. For the first time Roger was aware of a third person in the room.

Sprawled back in the easy chair, mouth open, a faint snore coming rhythmically, was Dr. Whales. In a flash Roger remembered one thing that had slipped his mind; the autopsy report on Perce Sheldon; that seemed to belong to an earlier age.

"Has he reported?" asked Roger, quietly.

"Sheldon died of digitalis poisoning," Kebble stated. "It was almost certainly from an injection in the right buttock."

Roger said: "So now we know. Anything in about Doreen Morrison?"

"She's under sedation. The Divisional Surgeon thinks she'll be able to talk tomorrow. She's not injured or harmed physically, and she's had plenty to eat, he says." Kebble was looking at Roger as if puzzled.

"Good," Roger said. "Hong Kong?"

"The call should be through any minute." Kebble paused, and then asked: "Care for a drink, sir?"

"Do I look as if I need it?"

"*I* do," Kebble said, rather awkwardly.

"Help yourself and pour me a double." Roger sat on the corner of his own desk, looking down at Whales. "Jessup killed himself," he announced unemotionally.

Kebble drew in a long, hissing breath, as if suffering from physical pain. He didn't speak; he had a gift for knowing when not to. He handed Roger a whisky and soda; he hadn't spared the whisky. Roger drank. Whales snored. Kebble sipped. Roger moved slowly and held his glass under Whales's nose. Whales's snore became brisker. His lips and nostrils twitched. Roger didn't move. The pathologist stirred, and his eyes flickered open. He squinted down at the glass, then hoisted himself back in his chair.

"Don't tempt me," he said. "When it sends me to sleep, I've had enough."

"Sure?"

"Yes," said Whales. He gave an involuntary shiver. "Bloody cold in here. Had the report?"

"Yes, thanks."

"Got a nice job on your hands, you have," said Whales. "Do something for me."

"Yes, gladly."

The flabby man grinned.

"No one quite like Handsome West," he said, glancing at Kebble. "Never has been, never will be. 'Yes' he says, although I might ask him for the moon. Send a driver to take me home, Roger."

"Fix it, will you?" Roger asked Kebble.

When both men had gone, five minutes later, he sat on the arm of the big chair. Big Ben, sounding very loud on the quiet night, began to chime the hour. It was midnight, and this case hadn't really got under way until about four o'clock this afternoon. He stretched, stood up, went to the window, and looked out at the lights of Westminster Bridge, lights from the old-fashioned lamps reflecting on the calm water of the Thames. Big Ben had a yellow glow, like a sickly man in the moon. The shape of the clock tower showed dark against the starlit sky; so did the shape of the rest of the Houses of Parliament.

Mother of Parliaments.

A telephone bell rang. He turned quickly, Parliament forgotten; this might be the Hong Kong call. He stepped towards the telephone as his door opened and Kebble appeared. Roger felt an impulse to wave to Kebble to take the call, but changed his mind. He lifted the receiver.

"Your call to Police Headquarters in Hong Kong, sir," the operator said.

"Hong Kong," Roger whispered to Kebble, who went across to pick up an extension. "Put me through."

"It's Superintendent Hodges on the line, sir."

Roger's heart leapt, for Hodges had once been a member of the Metropolitan Force. It was always helpful to speak to an old friend.

"Fred?" he said, a little too loudly.

"Hi, Handsome." Hodges sounded as clear as if he were in London. "You must be in serious trouble to spend money like water on telephone calls."

"That's right," Roger said. "Do you know anything about the death of a man—a ship's officer named Sanderson, of the S.S. *Kookaburra?*"

There was hardly a moment's pause.

"Yes, I know plenty about it," Hodges answered. "He was killed on the way back to his ship, knocked over the head, we thought, and pushed into the harbour near the Star Ferry. It took us three days to discover that he died of an injection of digitalis. We haven't a clue as to who did it, or why. Don't say you have."

Roger hesitated before he said: "I haven't, Fred, but I've two victims of the same poisoning here—passengers off the same ship. I don't like it much, do you?"

"My God I don't!" With hardly a pause, Hodges went on: "We'll split our sides here to try to find the killer. And I'll airmail you a full report today. Anything else?"

"Not yet," Roger said, almost awkwardly.

"Don't let it get you down," Hodges cracked. "See you one of these fine days, I hope."

"Next time you're on leave, come and spend a night or two at Bell Street," Roger invited.

When he rang off, he sat very still for some time. Kebble didn't move. Finally Roger looked across at him, raised his hands, and let them flop on to the desk.

"So there's another murderer as well as our missing man."

"Obviously no one who was on that ship is safe." Kebble spoke dispassionately, but nothing could take the cold horror out of his words.

"We'd better cable the Sydney Bureau," Roger said. "Tell 'em as much of the story as we can in a cable." He picked up a pencil. "Then we'd better get home."

"Like me to word the cable?" Kebble offered.

"If I don't like the wording in the morning, I'd rather blame myself," Roger said. He forced a smile. "You now see the rewards of promotion, don't you?"

Kebble said quietly: "Yes, sir, I see the reward of being on top of your job."

It was half past one when Roger turned the car into Bell Street, Chelsea, and then parked in front of the garage by the side of the house. The gates were open but the garage doors shut; neither of his sons had thought to open them for him. The late teens was a forgetful age. He pulled up within an inch of the doors, irritated, and walked on the grass alongside a concrete path to the back of the house. The back door was locked. He used his own key, making as little noise as he could. Although Janet slept at the front, trifling sounds disturbed her when he was not home. He switched on the light. On the kitchen table was a dish of sandwiches inside a plastic bag, instant coffee already in a cup, cream by its side. He lit the gas under the kettle. He had not realized he was so hungry until he tucked in. By the time the kettle was boiling, only one sandwich was left and his mood was already better.

The passage floor creaked.

The sound reminded Roger vividly of the creaking door at

the house in Notting Hill Gate. He started, and stared at the door, which was ajar. It moved under gentle pressure, and Richard's dark head appeared. Richard was a year younger than his brother, two inches taller, much more slender. His eyes looked huge with tiredness.

"Hi, Dad."

"What's the matter with sleep tonight?"

"I've been reading."

"Until *this* hour?"

"Jolly good book." Richard came farther in. He wore a suit of pale-blue pyjamas, much mended, gaping open to reveal a tanned chest. "True crime and all that. Had any luck?"

"My luck's right out," Roger answered. "Someone forgot to open the garage for me."

"Oh, damn!" Richard looked really contrite. "I knew there was something I meant to do. Sorry."

Roger's exasperation vanished.

"Try to remember, old chap."

"Yes, of course." Richard went to a bowl of fruit on the kitchen table, picked off a few green grapes, and ate them one by one. "I mean, about that girl in the paper—Scoop was talking about it just before he went to sleep. Is it going to be one of the big cases?"

"I wouldn't be surprised," Roger admitted.

"Beastly swine." Richard's vehemence made his lean cheeks flush and his tired eyes spark. "The devil who did it, I mean. What makes a man a murderer, Dad?" When Roger didn't answer at once, the lad went on: "I mean, could it happen to me? Could I be one?" When Roger still didn't answer Richard went on with a kind of restrained vigour: "I mean, people say 'but for the grace of God there go I'. Does it really mean every one of us is a killer at heart, only we don't all get the chance?"

It was nearly two o'clock, and even with a whole evening in front of him, Roger wouldn't have found it easy to answer those impassioned questions satisfactorily. Yet to make light of it, to be casual or uninterested, would not only be cruel but might discourage his son from asking questions of vital importance to them both.

"I don't think it means that," Roger said at last. "I don't think all human beings are potential murderers. I do think there are some with a bad streak in them, and others who learn to be callous. Can you kill and skin a rabbit?"

"You know I can."

"Can Scoop?"

Richard frowned, drawing his dark eyebrows together.

"He hates it if anyone kills a rabbit or anything near him."

"So there's something different in your make-up. People have such differences to a greater or lesser degree. The murderer with a bad streak is at one end of the scale. The boy who hates killing by hunting is at the other. Most of us are somewhere in between. Does that make it clearer?"

"I suppose so," Richard conceded. "I'm still a bit confused, though. Do you mean that because I can kill a rabbit and Scoop can't, I'm closer to being a murderer than he is?"

Roger almost groaned.

"No, I don't." He drank his coffee slowly. "I don't think this is the right end of the day to try to explain, but——"

"No, it isn't, and you look fagged out. I might be clearer on it in the morning, anyhow." Richard flashed a smile. "I hope so, anyway! 'Night, Dad. Sorry about the garage doors."

He went off.

Roger felt strangely light-hearted when he went upstairs; Richard had done him a world of good. He crept into his bedroom. Light from a street lamp showed Janet in the middle of the bed, dark hair against white pillow, both arms and shoulders covered. She did not stir as he got undressed, but when he was in bed beside her, she moved her warm, soft body against his, and said with unexpected clarity:

"Have you got to get up early?"

"Not too early."

"That's good," she said, and was asleep again in a few seconds.

Roger lay for a while, anxiety and fears for other people drawn out of him. Soon, he fell asleep. He did not dream. He was not aware of Janet getting up, just after seven o'clock, of the boys talking outside the room, or of the other noises of the house or of the street. He lay sleeping in this bright room, their bedroom ever since they had married, and the first thing to disturb him was the harsh note of the telephone; it had been switched through to the bedroom, as it always was by night, and Janet had forgotten to switch it back to the main instrument downstairs. There was a clatter of footsteps before the bell stopped ringing here, although he could hear the less strident noise downstairs.

He shifted over and picked up this extension.

". . . must you wake him? He was in so late."

Kebble's voice was unmistakable.

"I'm sure he would want to be called, Mrs. West."

"Oh, all right." Janet wasn't pleased, and did not hesitate to make it obvious. "Wait a minute." She let the telephone clatter and hurried to the foot of the stairs. "Scoop!" she called. "Wake your father and tell him Detective Sergeant Kebble says he must speak to him urgently."

"Right, Mum!" Almost at once, the door opened and Martin-called-Scoopy came in, broad face bright with excitement, broad, solid, eager. "Dad——"

Roger turned his head and winked.

"Oh, he's *awake*," Martin called down, in a tone of mock disgust. He advanced into the room as Roger waved the receiver.

"Yes, Kebble?"

"Sorry to disturb you, sir," Kebble said. "I thought you ought to know that there is a telephone call coming through from Sydney, New South Wales, at half past eight. That's half past six in the evening, their time. It's in response to your cable. Will you take the call at home, sir, or come to the office?"

The clock on Roger's bedside table pointed to five minutes to eight; so there was just time to get to the Yard.

9

CALL FROM AUSTRALIA

MARTIN-CALLED-SCOOPY'S eyes were as huge as Richard's had been the previous night, with a kind of earnest appeal, as if he divined the significance of the question. There were quiet footsteps on the stairs, and Janet appeared, hair wavy but tidy, without make-up except for a little lipstick, eyes bright with anxiety which she sensed rather than understood.

"You're going to have a good breakfast!" she whispered. "You can't work on an empty stomach."

Roger found himself grinning.

"Have it put through here, Keb, will you?"

"Right you are." If Kebble felt disappointed, he kept any trace of it out of his voice. "I'll fix it with the overseas operator. They didn't say who would call—the operator just said Sydney Criminal Investigation Bureau."

"With a bit of luck it will be Luke Shaw," Roger said. "What are you doing up so bright and early?"

"I got in at half past seven, seeing that it was bound to be a busy day."

"Had breakfast?"

"No, just a cuppa——"

"Go and have a good one," Roger said. He was smiling at Janet, who had come farther into the room. "You can't work on an empty stomach."

"Er—right, sir." Kebble sounded bewildered.

"Thanks for calling," Roger said, and rang off.

Janet said: "Beast," but came across, sat on the side of the bed and looked down at Roger, as if looking for some tell-tale sign. "You don't look as if you were up all night, I must say. Scoop, go and make some tea, and——"

"Char coming up!" That was Richard, from the stairs.

"I don't know what you two think you're going to worm out of me this morning," Roger said. "It's a hundred to one you won't succeed. There's a call from Sydney, Australia, coming through in half an hour. Run a bath for me, Scoop. Go down and check the car levels, Fish."

"Any orders for me?" demanded Janet.

Roger squeezed her hand.

"There's no time," he said, wickedly. "I'll be ready for that hearty meal at about a quarter to nine, though."

It was eight thirty-one; no call had come.

It was eighty forty-one; no call had come.

"I'm beginning to think you might wait for an hour. I'll cook your eggs," Janet said. "You boys ought to be on your way." They were rising twenty and rising nineteen, but still 'you boys' to Janet, particularly when she was preoccupied.

Martin was studying at an art school, not far away from Bell Street. Richard, longing for the day when he would be able to join a television company, the dream of his life, worked at a West End bookshop.

"If you don't go now you'll be late," Janet said. "No, Scoop, don't make me cross. I——"

The telephone bell rang. Roger strolled towards the main instrument, which was in the hall just outside the kitchen door. Roger lifted it, feeling that he was dramatizing a long-distance call simply because it impressed the boys. There was something else; a sense of foreboding, or at least of disquiet. Sydney could not have received the cable more than three or four hours ago. What made it so urgent for them to telephone halfway across the world so soon?

"This is Superintendent West of New Scotland Yard."

"Are you expecting a call from Sydney, Australia, caller?"

"Yes."

"Hold on, please."

Roger waited for what seemed a long time, and the others fussed and fidgeted about him, Janet pretending to be very busy in the kitchen. Suddenly a man said clearly:

"Mr. West?"

"Speaking," Roger said carefully.

"Good on you, Handsome!" The voice was loud, vigorous, unmistakably Australian. "How are things going with you?"

Roger smiled broadly.

"I'm fine, Luke. And you?"

"Never better, Handsome, never better!" Luke Shaw, who had been on a tour of Scotland Yard only two years before, was now Senior Superintendent in the Sydney C.I.B. He spoke as if he had never heard of a cable, and had all the time in the world. "How's that lovely wife of yours?"

"Wonderful!"

"You've said it, she always was." It was easy to imagine Shaw's big, broad face and beaming smile. "It's a good thing she is, because in every other way you like trouble, don't you?"

"Kookaburra trouble?" asked Roger.

"My word, yes. I can tell you all about it if you'll fly here and see me."

Roger was astonished enough to exclaim:

"Stop fooling!"

"I'm not fooling," Luke Shaw declared. A hint of laughter vanished from his voice. "Do you remember a ship called the S.S. *Koala*?"

"Should I?"

"Yes," said Shaw. "You certainly should. What happened to that could also happen to the *Kooka*." He halved the name abruptly. "Take it from me, Handsome, the only way for you to finish this job properly is to come out here."

"I don't think there's a ghost of a chance," Roger hedged. "At the moment I can't even see any reason. We've arrested one man who——"

"This Jessup—what's he like?" interrupted Shaw, and then began to answer his own question. "Five feet six, thin dark hair, pale face, very dark eyes, small mouth——"

"How the devil do you know?"

"Hold it, Handsome. Or is he six feet one, very big with a swarthy, pitted face? Which one?"

"The five foot six one," Roger answered in a subdued voice.

"He's no more Jessup than you're Luke Shaw. He's Paul Barring. The big man is his brother, Marcus. There's a third brother—Solomon. It's a hell of a long story, that's why I say that the best chance you've got of learning it is to come to Sydney." Shaw's voice boomed over the telephone.

"Why don't you come here?" countered Roger.

"Not a hope. Wouldn't do much good if I did. You need to know the background, get all the details, see all the records. Have a go, Handsome. You could do with some sunshine, couldn't you? If you need something to twist the arm of your boss, remind him that the *Kookaburra*'s nearer Australia than it is England, and when she docks you can start asking all the right questions." After a pause, he went on: "That is, if she docks. Her sister ship didn't make it."

That was the moment when Roger remembered what had happened to the S.S. *Koala*.

He did not speak at once; shock ran through his body, making him cold and still. He was not aware of Janet and the boys staring at him, touched by the tension which this recollection brought to him. He did not hear Richard say, whispering:

"What do you think's happened?"

In Roger's mind's eye there was a picture so vivid, so hideous in its wastage of human life, that he felt as if the breath had been drawn out of his body and he could not move or speak.

"So you get the angle," Luke Shaw said finally.

Roger gulped.

"Yes, I've remembered what happened to the S.S. *Koala*. She went down off the coast of Queensland a year or two ago with a loss of eighty-one passengers and twenty-odd crew. There were only a few survivors. Am I right?"

"My word you're right!" Shaw's voice seemed to vibrate in Roger's ear. "Know what worries me, Handsome? The same thing could happen to *Kookaburra*. She's got twelve cabin passengers, eighty-seven steerage, mostly Chinese from Hong Kong, and a crew of twenty-eight. And let me tell you something. The two Barring brothers were among the survivors of the *Koala*. They'd had their own line but were bought up by Blue Flag, after being driven almost out of business. There was a lot of bad blood between the Barrings and Blue Flag, and we've had an eye on the Barrings for some time but couldn't get anything on them. You've got plenty on one. What about the other?"

"If he's the man I think he is, he's loose in London," Roger stated.

"After killing two passengers, eh? Let me tell you something else. Solomon Barring was in Hong Kong when the *Kookaburra* was berthed there. Funny thing about Neil Sanderson's death, wasn't it? Handsome, if you can put the darbies on Marcus Barring, every policeman in New South Wales will drink your health. I'll put a detailed report on the first jet from the Kingsford Smith Airport this morning. Cable or call me with any news, won't you?"

"I will. Luke, have you any positive evidence that the *Kookaburra* might be in danger?"

"No," answered Shaw. "Just a nasty feeling. See you, Handsome."

He rang off, as if he was anxious to leave Roger to think on the situation.

Roger put the receiver down slowly, then ran his fingers through his hair. He was oblivious of the others until Richard broke the silence.

"How bad is it, Dad?"

Roger frowned, looked at them all, forced a smile, and answered:

"I should know before the night's out." It was really no answer at all, and it would not have surprised him had Richard tried to force the issue. A noise at the front door broke the tension; a newspaper appeared in the letter-box. Janet moved back to the kitchen, saying:

"Get the paper for your father, Richard. Breakfast in ten minutes, Roger. Scoop, you won't learn to be an artist by standing and gaping like that." She bustled about and set them all bustling, but the relief from tension did not last for long—hardly long enough for Roger to begin to digest the fact that Luke Shaw and the Sydney Police had no doubt of the enormity of the danger in this situation. He needed time to think, to absorb facts, to acquire more facts.

Could he do that, here in England? The first vague hope of a trip to Australia formed in his mind.

"Hey, look!" Richard broke the pipe dream. "Pop's hit the front page again."

Frying eggs, art school, and a bookshop were all forgotten as Richard came rushing along the passage, eyes blazing, *Daily Globe* spread out in his hands. Janet and Martin closed on him. All three read the headlines and then the story of what had happened last night, and saw the photographs of Roger and Doreen Morrison, with an inset picture of her dead sister.

"You saved her life," Richard said, humbly.

"He could easily have lost his own," said Janet, acidly. She turned on her heel and stamped back to the stove.

Roger saw the over-solemn look in the eyes of both boys, felt a moment's unease because there was no doubt of the hero-worship in them. He waved them away with a shooing motion of his hands, then tiptoed towards Janet. The boys went out the front way. Roger slid his arms round Janet's waist as she cracked an egg on the side of the frying-pan.

"No, I'm serious," she said, still sharp-voiced. "Why does it always have to be you risking your life?"

"Lots of others do it. You just happen to notice me," Roger replied. He squeezed more tightly, and put his cheek against hers. "Would you have liked me to let her die?"

"Don't be a fool, of course I wouldn't." Janet tipped the pan to let the boiling fat spread over the eggs, then turned round swiftly, taking his arms, gripping them. "Roger, every time something like this happens I feel scared in case—in case it's the last time your luck will hold."

She meant every word she said.

He leaned forward and kissed her.

"You're all the luck I need," he said gently.

Tears filled her eyes for a moment, she sniffed and pulled herself free. Before he left, half an hour later, she was brisker and brighter, but he knew she hadn't really recovered from her mood of fear.

Kebble was in the office. The morning post and reports had been sorted out and were in neat piles on Roger's desk. A third pile, of small pieces of paper, was of notes of telephone calls. Roger put his hat on a peg, and loosened his collar and tie. It was a bright, pleasant but chilly morning.

"Tired of life as a detective sergeant, are you?" Roger asked. "Prefer a desk of your own?"

Kebble grinned.

"As soon as you think I'm ready for it."

"You'll do." Roger dropped into his chair. "Did you get a tape of the talk I had with Sydney?"

"Yes, and I've listened to it. It's being transcribed now." Kebble, suddenly serious, reminded Roger of his own two sons. "How well do you know Superintendent Shaw, sir?"

"He's no scaremonger. You can take him at his word." Roger picked up the first telephone messages. The Commander C.I.D. wanted to see him. The laboratory had diagnosed the contents of the broken hypodermic needle as a concentrated solution of digitalis. Lancelot Smith of the Blue Flag Line had telephoned twice, but would leave no message. There were several other messages, none to do with the *Kookaburra* case. The news editor of the *Globe* had called twice.

"Anything in about the man who escaped from me last night?" Roger asked.

"He's not been caught," Kebble said. "He shared a room downstairs in the same house with the dead man. He gave his name as Jessup, too. Looks as if he really is the Marcus Barring Sydney talked about. The knife is of Australian make, probably used for wood carving. Some odd pieces of wood and some shavings were found in the room. They'd been at the house for four weeks. The two Morrison girls had that room you saw, and Denise went away about two weeks ago. According to the landlady, Doreen stayed on because she believed her sister would come back. Doreen hardly ever went out. The landlady is one of the 'ask no questions and you'll hear no lies' kind. The Division will have another go at her, but they think she's the type who doesn't care what happens provided she gets her rent."

The type wasn't uncommon.

"If necessary we'll talk to the lady herself," Roger said. "Any news of Doreen Morrison?"

"She should be able to talk this afternoon," Kebble answered. "There's a report on Limm, too. He's still in London."

Roger's telephone rang before he could ponder that information, and he lifted the receiver at once.

"There's a Mr. Lancelot Smith on the line," the operator said.

"I'll talk to him."

"Just a moment, sir."

It was only a moment, and when Smith spoke it was as if he had been stemming a flood of words but now they were released nothing could hold them back.

"Superintendent, I tried to call you earlier, I have some

news which was not in my possession last night. About the passengers who were on the *Kookaburra,* I mean. Mr. and Mrs. Parrish rejoined the ship at Marseilles. They are still on board and due to disembark at Sydney in ten days' time. I have Mr. and Mrs. Donelli's address. They have just written to inquire about sailings back to Sydney. They are in Naples, living with a married daughter. I have no trace, no trace at all of Mr. Samuel Hackett, but I understood he would move about the Continent with no set plan. I do know that he intended to visit Scandinavia and Germany as well as Switzerland because he asked us for information about those places. We referred him to Thomas Cook's nearest office. Can you—can *you* trace him, sir? After what I see in the newspapers this morning about the attempt to kill Miss Doreen Morrison, I feel that there is no end to the danger, no end at all."

The spate of words dried up.

"Mr. Smith," said Roger, "why didn't you tell me that the third officer was really Paul Barring, not Jessup? And do you know where I can find his brother Marcus?"

10

ADMISSION

"No, I've no idea where Marcus Barring is," Lancelot Smith declared. He sat in Roger's office, an hour after the telephone call, looking as heavy and gross-featured as he had the previous night, and tired as if he had not slept. "I did not know for certain that they were the Barrings. The Captain of the *Kookaburra* had no idea, either. Both men left the ship at Southampton, and one of the crew said he thought they were two of the Barring brothers. I didn't know, Superintendent."

Roger was stony-eyed.

"Was the taller brother accused of theft?"

"No. He was ship's carpenter and handyman, not an officer. He told the first officer that he was leaving the ship as a protest because of the charges of theft made against his brother."

"Why didn't you tell me about the loss of the *Koala*?" Roger demanded.

"I wondered if I should. I did indeed. But I wavered between loyalty to my employers and—and my duty to the police. I did not wish to revive the old stories, the old scandals. The Barrings always believed their company had been ruined by the Blue Flag line, and—but it is a long, long story. I know only a little of it. I sent a long cable to my owners in Sydney last night asking permission to give you all details. I expect a reply today. Even so I cannot see that I have done any harm, Mr. West."

"I hope you haven't," Roger said bleakly. "Have you the Donellis' address?"

"Yes." Smith took a slip of paper from his pocket.

"Thanks. I'll do all I can to protect them," Roger promised. "I don't yet know what I can do about the Parrishes. Is there anything else you can tell me about Samuel Hackett?"

"I only wish there were," Smith said.

Old Sam Hackett seemed to be having the time of his life in Paris. A man was only as old as his hopes, and Paris gave him a lot to hope for. The few acquaintances he had made, the staff at the little hotel near the Madeleine where he was staying, and the quite attractive 'girl' in her middle thirties who had a soft spot for the old man who was so delighted she was ready to share her divan with him, all felt sure that he had entered a new lease of life.

Lancelot Smith had been gone for an hour. Roger had read through all the reports. Limm had gone to a theatre the previous night, by himself, and gone to his hotel, also by himself.

A general call had gone out to all Divisions, Home Counties forces, and all ports and airports for a man answering Solomon Barring's description; no photograph of Barring was available.

Roger went along to see his chief, Commander Hardy, a man whom he had known for many years, who had risen from the ranks, and who was still not always easy in the seat of authority. It was seldom possible to be absolutely sure whether he would approve or disapprove of any action taken. Spread over his desk were the morning newspapers, with the *Globe* prominent among them.

"Good morning," Roger said.

Hardy grunted.

"'Morning. Any further developments on this digitalis job?"

"Nothing good or worth worrying you about."

"It all worries me," Hardy said. "The New South Wales people seem to think it might be connected with the loss of a ship two years ago. Can you see any connection between a ship which foundered in the Pacific Ocean and a madman running around killing people in London?"

"Madman?" Roger echoed.

"That's what he looks like to me. Very bad thing that Jessup—*alias* Barring—killed himself. Can't blame you for that but someone will try to sooner or later. Worried about the other passengers?"

"Very."

"So am I," said Hardy. "Especially those in this country. Drop anything else you're doing and concentrate on this, Handsome. You have *carte blanche*." He gave a wintry smile. "Not too many heroics, though. If I had to choose between having you alive or these other people alive I'd settle for you."

He nodded dismissal. Roger, who hadn't sat down, felt curiously deflated; Hardy in some moods had that effect. Hardy's telephone rang, and Roger went out. By the time he was back in his office, he was feeling more satisfied. He had a free hand

and could concentrate on the *Kookaburra* case; only now did he realize how much he wanted to do that. The feeling of disquiet which had been in his mind from the beginning of the case was as strong as ever. It was not only because one of the Barrings was loose in London, likely to kill again; it was something he could not quite grasp, a feeling that there was a hidden factor which he should be able to see but could not.

Kebble was talking on the telephone. Roger picked up a new note from his own desk. It read:

Doreen M came round at 11.45 a.m.

He picked up his own telephone, and called the Yard's chief liaison with *Interpol*.

"Yep?" The other superintendent liked talking in monosyllables.

"Jay, I want to find an elderly Australian, named Hackett, who is somewhere in Europe having a good time. He was on the *Kookaburra*, and——"

"Wondered when you'd want some help on that," the other interrupted. "Any idea where the old geezer is?"

"I'll send a note of all I've got. And there's a Mr. and Mrs. Donelli——" Roger gave a brief description of the Donellis, and went on: "Try to persuade the Naples police that this is serious, will you?"

"They won't take much convincing."

"Thanks." Roger rang off, to find Kebble off his telephone and making notes. "Got all that?" Kebble, scribbling, nodded. "Give Interpol everything we've got," Roger said. "I'm going to see the Morrison girl."

Hardy had in fact done him good. He felt fit and more confident as he ran down the Yard's steps, and across to his car. The presentiment was forgotten. A C.I.D. woman was by Doreen's bedside, and would take notes; he could drive himself. The sun warmed him. Blessedly, there was no interference from the Yard by radio. He found a parking space almost opposite the nursing home where the girl had been taken; it was one used a great deal by the Yard, and the atmosphere was conducive to interviews with witnesses. He wondered how much Doreen knew or would tell him, then realized belatedly that he would probably have to break the news of her sister's death. He saw a man coming down the four steps which led from the front door.

It was Benjamin Limm, the first man to identify Denise Morrison. He was glowering, and did not recognize Roger at first.

"Good morning," Roger said.

Limm started back, and recognition dawned. He stopped squarely in front of Roger, as if spoiling for a fight.

"You've no right to keep Miss Morrison here against her will."

"How did you know where to find her?" Roger demanded.

"I asked the *Globe*. They gave me a hell of a lot of trouble. Bloody pommies," Limm went on raspingly. "She wants to get out of this goddammed country, the quicker the better. And if you try to stop her I'll see the High Commissioner. If necessary I'll fly home and see the Prime Minister."

"Take it easy," Roger said. "No one wants to keep anyone here against his will. Have you seen her?"

"Yes."

"How did you get in?"

"I said I was a relation, and they let me in. She looks awful. All she wants to do is get out of this country——"

"Yes, you said that before," Roger interrupted. "It might have been as well if you and the others had not come in the first place, there's no profit in the export of murder." That stopped Limm in full flood. "I'm going to see her. If you're in a better mood when I come out we might talk. Like to sit and wait in my car?"

Limm, still nonplussed, asked: "How long will you be?"

"Half an hour or so."

"I'll come back."

"Limm," Roger said, "did you know the ship's carpenter on the *Kookaburra*, a man who called himself Marcus Jessup?"

Limm caught his breath. "What about him?"

"He may be after your life," Roger said. "Keep your eye open for him."

He left Limm standing. A man across the road raised a newspaper; he was the Yard man watching Limm, there was little danger. Roger went up to the front door. A young girl opened it, an elderly woman came to escort him up to Doreen Morrison's room. Even halfway up the stairs the sound of shouting, with an unmistakable note of hysteria, was audible.

"She was very excitable soon after she woke," the Sister said. "And the visit from her cousin made her much worse."

"Does she know about her sister?" Roger asked.

"Yes—*he* told her."

"Oh, did he," Roger said heavily. "No wonder she was worse."

The Sister opened the door of a room on the right. It was small and rather gloomy, with light coming only from one small window set high in the wall. A nurse was holding Doreen's hands, the C.I.D. woman was standing in a corner, looking on. Her expression seemed to say: "Leave her to me, I'll knock the nonsense out of her."

Roger's impression of the girl was very different from what he had expected. The hysteria had put glowing red into Doreen's cheeks, and made her blue eyes spark and glitter. She looked quite lovely.

"I don't want to stay here. I want to go back home. I don't care what you say. I hate it here!" She leaned forward and glared at Roger. "Perhaps *you* can make them see sense!" she cried.

"Perhaps you'll see some sense yourself when you know that this man saved your life last night—and saved it twice." The C.I.D. woman looked and spoke like a severe headmistress. "Why he should risk his own to save yours God only knows. *I* don't."

Doreen Morrison stopped glaring, stopped trying to free herself from the nurse's restraining hands. She sat quite upright, still very lovely even though the colour faded from her cheeks and the fire in her eyes slowly died.

Roger smiled gently.

"Hallo, Miss Morrison. I'm glad to see you looking better." He moved forward and shook hands; and when he went on his voice was pitched very low. "And I am desperately sorry about your sister."

Doreen's eyes filled with tears. She sat there, clutching Roger's right hand, gulping, trying to fight back a gust of crying. But she could not. She leaned forward against Roger, sobbing desperately, piteously. No one seemed to move, although the paroxysm seemed to last for a long time.

At last, the tears slackened. Soon, she eased her body away from Roger's, and looked round as if for a handkerchief. The nurse had a towel handy. Doreen dabbed her swollen, reddened eyes, sniffed, tried to speak, failed, and tried again.

"I do want to go home," she said miserably. "I can't stand it in England without Denise. I really can't. Help me, please help me."

Very quietly, Roger said: "When you've told us everything you can and given us the help we need, you can go home. That's a promise."

It took some time for the import of what he said to register. Then radiance lighted up those reddened eyes, before they filled with tears again.

Soon, she asked: "How long must I stay here?"

"Not very long."

"A day? A week? A month?"

"Less than a week, if all goes well," Roger said. "I'm going to ask you just one question, then I've work to do while you tell the detective sergeant here all you can."

She nodded. "What's the question?" she asked.

"How well do you know Ben Limm?"

"Not—not really well. He was on the *Kookaburra*. Denise —Denise liked him a lot."

"Did he like her?"

"I—I think so. I think he liked us both."

"Have you met him since you left the ship?"

"We had lunch the first day ashore, that's all," Doreen answered.

"Are you sure?"

"Of course I'm sure."

"Did your sister meet him in London?"

"Only at that lunch. She would have told me. I———" Doreen broke off and put her hands up in front of her face, as if to fend off some physical thing. "She might have met him after she went away. I don't know. She was away so long."

"Did you ever know a man named Brown—a friend of Denise?"

"No," Doreen said. "No, I didn't." There was new tension in her as she leaned forward again. "Why—why did you ask me about Ben? He's got nothing to do with this—he can't have."

That was the moment when Roger realized that the girl was in love with Benjamin Limm.

11

GIRL IN ANGER

BENJAMIN LIMM came striding along the pavement, a picture of restrained aggression, as Roger left the nursing home. The Yard man tailing the Australian was at the corner. Roger half expected to be greeted truculently, but instead Limm was surprisingly mild mannered.

"How is she?"

"No worse," Roger said. "I want to talk to you. Get in my

car." He went to the door and opened it. After a moment's hesitation Limm got in. Roger sat next to him. Before starting the engine he flicked on the radio.

"This is Superintendent West," he said to *Information*. "I want inquiries made at the *Globe* to find out whether anyone on the paper told a Mr. Benjamin Limm where to find Miss Doreen Morrison——"

"I can save you time," Limm interpolated. "I saw the deputy news editor."

"Try the deputy news editor first," Roger went on.

Information said: "Right away, sir. Will you talk to Detective Sergeant Kebble?"

"Yes."

"One moment, please."

After at least a minute, Kebble came on the line. All the time Limm stared intently at Roger, without attempting to speak.

"I had a message from Lancelot Smith," Kebble said without preamble. "He confirms that a supply of digitalis in capsule form was on the *Kookaburra*. It was for a passenger two trips earlier, and the surplus was never removed from the Medical Cupboard."

"Another nail," Roger said. "Anything else?"

"A man answering Marcus Barring alias Jessup's description left London Airport on the 10.15 flight to Düsseldorf and places East," answered Kebble. "He had a ticket through to Sydney but said he wanted to break his journey at Düsseldorf and Hong Kong. He had one suitcase, and his ticket was booked under the name of Brown."

"Brown!" ejaculated Roger. "The name Denise Morrison was registered under when she was found. What time does the plane leave Düsseldorf?"

"Twelve-ten," answered Kebble. "I've asked the Superintendent on Interpol to find out if he left the aircraft at Düsseldorf."

"Where's the next stop?"

"Istanbul, at about six o'clock, then Teheran about ten. I've briefed the Superintendent."

"Keep at it," Roger said. "More?"

"Not yet!"

"Take these notes, I keep forgetting them," Roger said. "Have a memo written to the department and the Division concerned. The switchboard operator on duty last night—the one who took the call from Doreen Morrison—was too excitable, but very quick. She wants to be calmed down a bit, nicely. The policeman who saved me from a lot of trouble at Notting Hill ought to get a commendation. And make a note for me to have a word with him some time."

Almost at once, Kebble said: "His name was Harris, C. P. Harris. I'll fix it, sir."

"Good," said Roger. "I should be back in half an hour and I may or may not have Benjamin Limm with me. I've promised Doreen Morrison I will take her statement personally, some time this evening."

"Right."

"That's all," Roger said.

"Don't go, Super," put in another man on the line, "I've had a word with the deputy editor of the *Globe*. He did give that address to Limm. One of the *Globe* reporters should have been waiting when Limm left, but he was sent on to a smash-and-grab in Oxford Street."

"That'll be a relief to one man, anyhow. Thanks." Roger switched off and looked at Limm. "The *Globe* corroborated for you."

"The only thing that surprises me is you were so quick."

"We don't lose more time than we have to," Roger said. "Limm, do you know anything at all you haven't told us? Anything at all unusual which took place on the *Kookaburra,* for instance."

"No," answered Limm quietly. "I didn't see anyone— Denise or Doreen included—later than I told you. The last time was the lunch on the day we reached England. That's what you mean, isn't it?"

"I mean is there anything more you can tell us of any kind about the voyage."

"There was one thing," Limm said reflectively. "Jessup, who killed himself in his cell, was an officer on board. He was caught in passengers' cabins twice, and confined to his quarters on the last stage of the journey. I thought the shipping company would charge him with theft, but all they seem to have done was to fire him."

"Did he steal anything?"

"He had old Sam Hackett's wallet, crammed with currency, in his quarters. The old man was very decent about it. I happened to share a cabin with him and knew what was going on."

"Did Hackett tell you where he was going?" Roger was now weaving his way through the West End traffic, yet seemed oblivious of its complexity.

"He said he was going to go everywhere and do everything." Limm laughed. "He's a high-stepping old boy, and he's got no one to leave his money to. He didn't care how much he spent. He didn't go into any details, though."

"If you think of any chance remark, anything which might give us a clue about where to find him, let us know at once," Roger said.

"Think he's on the list?" asked Limm heavily.

"He could be," Roger said. "You could be, too. I'd have a lot more questions to ask any *Kookaburra* passenger who isn't on the list. As far as you know could anything which happened on board explain what is happening now?"

Without hesitation, Limm answered: "Absolutely nothing."

They were in St. James's Park now, nearing the Horse Guards Parade. Roger was silent for a minute or two, and Limm was about to speak when he said:

"Why this sudden interest in Doreen Morrison?"

"It's not all that sudden," Limm answered gruffly. "I always had a soft spot for her, but there was no hope of prising her from Denise, and I didn't try. Once I realized how she would feel over the murder, and what a mess she would be in, I had to try to help."

Roger didn't speak.

"That's the simple truth," Limm said awkwardly.

"I didn't question it."

"You question everything," Limm retorted, half angry, half admiring. "What about Doreen? Can she go home?"

"I don't see why not. With Paul Barring dead, we don't need her evidence of his attempt on her life. If her statement is straightforward and she undertakes to swear further depositions in Australia if required, I think it can be arranged. Sure you want to take her back?"

"Absolutely."

"Give me your London address and I'll keep in touch," said Roger. "But stay away from her until I give the word, will you?"

"Oh, all right," Limm promised. "That right you're going to take her statement yourself?"

"Yes."

"Quite the ladies' man, aren't you?" Limm half jeered.

When Roger reached the nursing home late that afternoon, Doreen was up and dressed, and looking much better. Curiously she had lost something of her attractiveness. A younger woman C.I.D. officer was with her, and she gave Roger the impression that she was very pleased with herself.

"Miss Morrison has made a statement voluntarily, sir."

"Oh," said Roger. He half wished this hadn't happened, he knew more than the officer was ever likely to know about a witness's facial expressions when making a statement; but it was done now. "Let me see it." As he took it he smiled at Doreen. "Is there anything you've remembered since you made this?"

"No, nothing," she answered.

Roger read the report, and within a few sentences his

dissatisfaction with the C.I.D. woman vanished; she must have phrased this, and she hadn't wasted a word. It read:

I, Doreen May Morrison, of Adelaide, South Australia, an Australian citizen lawfully holding Passport Number 851972, make this statement voluntarily and of my own free will.

On March 23rd of this year I reached Southampton on the S.S. *Kookaburra* after a journey from Australia which had lasted six weeks. I was with my sister, Denise. Our joint intention was to obtain work in England, to save sufficient money for a long tour of the Continent, and to return to Australia after twelve or eighteen months. At Southampton we were told by Jessup that we could obtain work at a certain office in London. We knew that Jessup had been accused of theft on the ship, but he told us that this was unjustified, and that he had been in passengers' cabins looking for property of his own. He did not say what property. I did not want to accept any favour from Jessup, but Denise was impressed by the salaries he said we were being offered—£20 sterling a week each—and we decided to go with him.

Jessup took us to a house in Notting Hill Gate, London, where the police afterwards found me. From the beginning the arrangement was unsatisfactory but for some reason why I never understood, Denise accepted it. I had an impression that she was influenced by Jessup's brother, Marcus, who had been one of the *Kookaburra*'s crew. We were told that the jobs had fallen through. I did some temporary work at garages in Hammersmith and Shepherd's Bush, and Denise obtained a part-time job as an assistant in a dress shop, but her work did not last long. I had reason to believe she was having an *affaire* with Marcus Jessup. The smaller brother, Paul, was extremely attentive to me, but I did not like him in spite of the fact that he (as well as his brother) appeared to have plenty of money. From time to time Paul Jessup asked me questions about how much I knew about him, and whether anyone on the ship had told us anything about him. I said no one had talked to me about him except after the thefts.

After two weeks, Denise left the rooms one morning, and did not come back. I did not see Marcus Jessup again after that, and believed they had gone off together. Paul told me that she would return. For a week I stayed at the rooms hoping she would. When I said that I would have to leave, Paul told me that I would never see Denise again unless I stayed there. Although he made frequent advances to me, he did not attempt to force himself on me. He promised me new clothes, jewellery, and anything I wanted if I would live with him. I refused. His questions about whether anyone had accused him of committing crimes became more and more insistent. I always told the truth, that no one had, but he did not appear to believe me.

One day (about five days before he made an attack on my life) I slept very heavily and when I came round I believed he had drugged me. From then on I was half dazed all the time. On one occasion I was awakened by a sharp pain in the arm, and saw Jessup holding a hypodermic syringe. I tried to get off the bed but he held me down until I lost consciousness. He kept telling me that if I didn't tell him what I knew about him I would never see Denise again. I woke up one afternoon, and he was not in the room. I dressed, although very tired, and went out. It was the first time I had been out of doors for nearly a week. I saw a newspaper on a hallstand downstairs, and picked it up. Denise's picture was on the front page. I knew something was badly wrong. I went to a telephone booth along the street and telephoned the number in the newspaper—Scotland Yard. I spoke to a man who said he was Superintendent West. He told me to stay where I was until he came to fetch me. Paul Jessup arrived first, however. I was frightened of him but tried to run away. He over-powered me, and forced me to go back to the rooms. Then he pinned me to the bed with his knee while he picked up a hypodermic syringe. He kept saying it was my fault, he didn't want to do it, but he had to. I believe he was going to kill me. Before he could give me the injection, however, another man arrived and stopped him. I was afterwards told that this man was Superintendent West. I remember nothing else until I woke up in a strange room. I was told that this was in a small nursing home, often used by the police. I know of nothing else relevant to this statement.

Roger was aware of the girl staring at him; and of the C.I.D. woman's gaze, as if in hopes of quick approval.

"Very concise," Roger said. "Just one or two questions, Doreen—mind if I call you Doreen?"

"Of course not."

"Did you ever hear the two Jessups talking about the *Kookaburra*?"

"No, never."

"Did Paul ever explain anything more about the accusations of theft?"

"No."

"Did you or Denise ask him about this?"

"I didn't, and I don't think Denise did—she didn't ever say so, anyhow." Doreen was quite composed when talking about her sister.

"Are you sure no one ever told you anything about Paul Jessup—something which might explain his insistence in questioning you?"

After a pause, as if she was trying to understand the full implications of the question, Doreen said:

"No one ever said anything—except about the thefts on board the ship."

"Did Paul ever say where he got his money from?" asked Roger.

"No."

"Although you were living in a very ordinary house in a poor quarter of London, did you believe he had plenty of money?"

"Yes. I saw his wallet, crammed full, more than once."

"Did he bring anyone else to see you?"

"No."

"Did you ever go out to meet any of his friends?"

"No."

"Didn't you think this strange?"

Doreen hesitated, but Roger did not prompt her.

"It didn't seem strange at first," she said. "I went out to work during the day, and in the evenings met Den and rushed off to see London. We couldn't see enough of it—we loved every bit. We went to places like Windsor and Hampton Court at week-ends—Den loved the green of the grass—she——"

The girl's eyes flooded with tears, but she fought them back, and went on:

"Some evenings we went out to a movie, or dozed, or watched television. It wasn't until Denise went away that it really seemed strange. Then I was too frightened to think about it. It was like a nightmare—waiting, waiting."

Now the tears spilled over.

When she had recovered, Roger asked quietly:

"Did the Jessups ever talk about Ben Limm?"

Immediately Doreen was on her guard.

"No, they didn't."

"Did Ben ever talk about them?"

"No!"

"Never?" asked Roger, still gently.

"He said he didn't trust them. He had lunch with us the day we got to London, and we told him what the Jessups were going to do. He tried to stop us. He said they couldn't be trusted out of sight. He seemed to hate them!"

"Did he say why?"

"It was because of the trouble on the ship. It must have been." For the first time since Roger had arrived hostility and suspicion were back in her manner—and again emotion touched her elfin face with unexpected beauty. "Why do you keep on about Ben?"

Roger answered almost before the question was out.

"Because all the other passengers on the *Kookaburra* who stayed in London have been attacked—except Benjamin Limm. Doesn't that strike you as odd?"

For a moment, Doreen looked shocked. Then anger flared in her eyes, and she jumped up and raised a clenched fist.

12

FLYING ORDERS

ROGER did not move or flinch. The girl's cheeks were fiery red and her blue eyes sparked with her anger. For a moment it looked as if she would strike him, but she stopped herself, lowered her arm, and swung away.

"No, I don't think it's odd. You've got it in for Ben for some crazy reason."

"Doreen——" began Roger.

"Don't call me Doreen!"

"Miss Morrison, whether you want to acknowledge it or not, it is most noteworthy that no one has shown any enmity towards Mr. Limm. If you blind yourself to that you will be very silly. You might endanger your life again."

She flared up again. "Why do you keep accusing Ben?"

"I'm trying to make you understand that you don't know him well enough to trust him implicitly," Roger answered. "You only met him on the ship."

"Anyone would think you knew he was a criminal!"

"I simply don't know enough about him yet," Roger said. "He may be, he probably is, everything he says he is. I hope that's how it turns out. But don't take him or anyone for granted until the whole truth is known."

Doreen was standing and facing him, her lips quivering.

"If you hadn't let Marcus Jessup get away you wouldn't have to try to find a scapegoat."

"No, I wouldn't, would I?" Roger said. "I can tell you one thing for certain."

"What's that?"

"Marcus Jessup—whose real name is Barring"—Roger paused long enough to judge whether that revelation meant anything to her, but she showed no sign—"has left London.

We think he is on his way to Australia. You might be safer in this country until he's caught."

Doreen drew a deep, shuddering breath.

"I hate this country! I want to get out, out, out! Don't you understand? I want to go *home*. The police there won't let such dreadful things happen. I want to go home!"

Roger picked up the statement from the bed, and handed it to her, together with a pen.

"Sign this," he said. "Then you will be free to go."

She put the paper on a small table; it rustled a little under her unsteady fingers but her signature was swift and firm. She handed it to him with an air of defiance which showed no sign of waning.

"If I were you I'd stay here for the night," Roger advised. "But please yourself. Mr. Limm will be here at about half past seven." He nodded, without smiling, and turned away. He half expected Doreen to call him back, but she did not.

Next morning he had a report that Limm visited the nursing home on time, had a meal there with Doreen, and left at about ten o'clock. There was a later report: that Limm had booked two economy class seats on a B.O.A.C. flight from London Airport to Sydney. The plane was due to leave at 10.15 on Monday in five days' time, and was due in Sydney on the Wednesday afternoon.

During the next two days there were no new developments of any significance. No news had come in about Sam Hackett, who was in fact having an incredibly wonderful time with his new light o' love in a small town in the Loire district. Sam appeared to be so enamoured that he might at any time propose marriage. He was seventy-seven, but nothing in his appearance or in his behaviour suggested he was a day over sixty.

The Parrishes, Jack and Jill, were enjoying the voyage back to Australia quite as much as they had enjoyed the one to

England. Life was still a honeymoon, a long, golden honeymoon. They had not even heard of what had happened to their fellow passengers in London. Even had they known that Marcus Jessup, alias Barring, was in Sydney waiting for the return of the ship, it would not have worried them; they were too happy, and completely unaware of danger. Jack Parrish was a tall, rangy Queenslander, lean-faced, full of vigour and vitality. Jill was nearly as tall, a handsome girl with a fine full figure who always ate a little too much. She was invariably cheerful. She worshipped her husband for his kindness, his humour, his devotion, and the grey flecks in his hair.

They were then twelve days out of Sydney.

On that particular day, the Friday before Doreen and Limm were to fly from London, it was very hot in Sydney, but dry and free from humidity. After a sticky late April, Sydneyites revelled in the day and began to hope that the weather would hold for the week-end. About five o'clock in the afternoon (seven o'clock in the morning in London, where Roger West was just getting up) Superintendent Luke Shaw of the Sydney C.I.B. sat signing the day's letters. He was a big, broad-faced man, who in repose could look almost dull, but in action had the speed and sharpness of a ferret.

There was a tap at his door, and it opened. He glanced up to see a young C.I.B. officer, in plain-clothes. It would have surprised Roger West to see such a caller, unheralded, in an office the equivalent to Hardy's. Shaw wasn't surprised; he kept an ever-ready ear open to all the staff.

"Come in, Dyson. What's on your mind?" The subject could be anything from troubles at home to troubles in the office, an unofficial report or a complaint about a senior officer.

"I've got a suggestion to make, sir, about the filing system in the Handwriting Section when we move to the new premises."

"Told Jack Clark about it?"

"He said to see you."

"What is it?" asked Shaw.

"Instead of filing with the new cases at the front and the old ones at the back, why not vice versa?" suggested Dyson. "Most references are to older cases—it would save time."

"I'll have a word with Jack, but don't run away with the idea that any department's going to have all the room they want when we move. They're converting an old factory, not putting up a new police palace like they do in the country towns such as Coffs Harbour." Shaw was half serious. "If it saves time it's all right with me, but I don't want any changes for the sake of change."

"I won't suggest any of that kind," Dyson assured him.

The telephone bell rang. Shaw picked it up as he waved Dyson away. Anyone who asked for him was put straight through; in Luke Shaw's book, formality was another word for loss of time.

"Shaw."

"*Luke* Shaw?" a man asked.

"Yes, this is Luke Shaw."

"*Superintendent* Luke Shaw?" the caller insisted.

Shaw frowned, the instinct for suspicion alert in him now. He shifted his position, pressed a bell for someone from outside to come in, and answered without any show of suspicion; there was a faint note of asperity in his voice, that was all.

"Yes, Superintendent Shaw speaking. Who is that?"

"You bloody coppers," the caller said. "You or the bloody pommies. You're going to get some shocks before this is over. Barring's back—Marcus Barring. You couldn't keep him out of the country, could you? The pommies couldn't keep him in theirs and you couldn't keep him out of ours. I'm telling you—he's spoiling for a fight."

The line went dead as a sergeant came in from next door. The sergeant stood very still, watching Shaw's face, understanding his senior officer so well that he did not need telling that this was no time to talk.

At last, Shaw spoke.

"Marcus Barring's in town. Put out an all-state alert." He banged the platform of the telephone up and down, and when the operator answered, he said sharply: "Get me Superintendent West of Scotland Yard.... Yes, London. Eh?" He scowled. "He'll be in his office around nine o'clock, I should say. I'll stay here until the call comes through." He put the receiver down and pressed a bell. A moment later an older, white-haired man came in—Shaw's deputy. "Mac, Marcus Barring's in town."

"You sure?" Mac asked, reflectively.

"We had a tip-off," Shaw replied, "and the squeaker knew what he was talking about. I want you to drop everything, and concentrate on this. Handsome West should be on the line in a couple of hours, be ready to listen-in on an extension."

Mac said: "My word I will." He smoothed down silky, snow-white hair, which with his pale, blemishless skin gave him something of the look of an albino. "I'd like one more thing, Luke."

"What's that?"

"Confirmation that Barring's here."

"Not satisfied?"

"Nor would you be if anyone else said so on the strength of one phone call. I'm prepared to bet you're right, but we still need proof."

"That's what we'll get if enough of our chaps keep their eyes open," Shaw retorted. He looked up at a tap at the door. "Come in." It was a youngish man, red-haired, bright-eyed. "What is it, Red? I'm busy right now."

"You're not too busy for this," the younger man said. "Here's a cable from West of the Yard." He came up to the desk and planted a handwritten note in front of Shaw. "Doreen Morrison and the man Limm are flying here early next week. West also says Marcus Barring has been traced as far as Bombay. They lost trace then. He could be in New South Wales by now."

Shaw nodded.

"I'll be talking to West in a couple of hours," he said. "If anything else comes in from the Yard, or there's any word about Barring, let me know. You right?"

"I'm right," Red said, and hurried out.

On that Friday morning Roger West arrived at the office just after eight o'clock. It was empty. He realized how accustomed he had become to seeing Kebble there. His desk was clear except for a couple of messages, put there recently. The morning's mail wasn't in yet, and his own desk was exactly as he had left it the previous night. As he sat down, loosening his collar, a telephone bell rang. He answered at once.

"West."

"I heard you were in," the operator said. "There's a call coming through from Sydney, New South Wales, sir. What time can you take it?"

"Any time," Roger said eagerly.

"It will be in about half an hour then. Will you stay in your office?"

"If I have to leave it I'll let you know where to find me."

"If you would, sir."

Roger put down the telephone, trying to discourage his rising excitement and an almost choky feeling of suffocation, an unreasoned presentiment which had been like a shadow over him from the beginning of this case. Again his mind flashed to the possibility of flying to Australia, but he set the thought firmly aside. He sat for a few seconds, then put in a call to *Information*.

"Who was watching Limm last night?"

"Detective Sergeant Scott, sir."

"Has he reported?"

"All was well at eight o'clock, when he was relieved by Detective Officer Warrender."

"And Miss Morrison?"

"The same, sir."

"Thanks," Roger said.

He went across to the window and looked out upon the Embankment. It was a grey, cheerless morning, with a spittle of rain in the air. The Thames was absolutely flat, rippling only when a string of barges or a motor-boat passed. He wondered what kind of sea the *Kookaburra* was sailing through. It could be rough down there among the islands. He moved across to the bookcase by the side of his desk, took down a thick Atlas, and turned to the Far East. The ship should be somewhere near the Philippines in the seas of countless islands, tropical heat, cyclones which could swallow up great ships.

It *should* be near there, but—was it?

If there was any trouble at all with the *Kookaburra*, word would come through in a few hours. In these days of swift communication ships didn't simply vanish without a trace.

A thought came to him, swift and blinding. He stood very still, poring over the page in the atlas. He turned abruptly, sat down and took up the file on the *Kookaburra* case, opened it, and thumbed it through. Kebble had prepared the file with his usual thoroughness. Roger came upon a smooth, shiny brochure with a white slip on it. *The Blue Flag Line Sailing Lists.* On the first page was a list of the ships of the line, and at the top the note:

> The Blue Flag Line is today a fleet of 27 modern cargo vessels, each of which carries passengers. Each ship sails from Australian Ports carrying Australian goods to all parts of the world. From the *Kangaroo*, the commodore ship of the line, twenty-two thousand tons gross with first-class accommodation for over 200 passengers to the *Kookaburra*, of seven thousand tons gross weight carrying 12 first-class passengers, the 27 ships have the best possible facilities for both passengers and cargo.

There followed a list of the ships. *Kangaroo, Blue Gem, Merino, Alice, Barbarossa* ... each one had some kind of Australian association although he was not aware of the full significance of it.

Somewhere on the Seven Seas ships of the Blue Flag Line were carrying precious cargoes. . . .

If this was a campaign of hate against the Blue Flag Line, why stop at the *Kookaburra*? Why stop at any one vessel? There were twenty-seven ships of the line.

His telephone bell rang. It seemed to rasp at him from some other world, jarring through the quiet of the office and the shocked stillness of his own mind. It rang again and again. When he lifted it there was asperity in the operator's voice.

"Oh, you *are* there. Your call from Australia."

"I'll take it."

"It's Superintendent Shaw."

"Thanks."

"Handsome," Shaw said. This time he seemed rather farther away, but his voice and his words were clear enough. "I've some news for you. Marcus Barring is here in New South Wales. It's positive now—he's been seen by two uniformed men, but they weren't able to pick him up. It looks as if he'll be waiting here—for the Parrishes and for the Morrison girl and Limm."

"Could be," Roger said. "Watch them closely, Luke."

"It's a hell of a problem," Shaw said. "We can't be sure there's any danger to anyone on the *Kookaburra,* and we can't be sure the *Kookaburra*'s in danger."

"We can't be sure which ship in the Blue Flag Line is in danger, can we?" asked Roger. "We've got to get Barring, we've got to get his missing brother Solomon. Luke, how about a man six feet tall, thirty-five or so, between-colours, grey eyes, slightly curly hair, full of vitality, very direct way of talking. Could that be Solomon Barring?"

"It could," answered Shaw, slowly. "Yes, it could."

"Check on Benjamin Limm, of Cowra——" began Roger.

"I'm checking," said Shaw. "It's just conceivable——" He broke off. "One thing's certain."

"What's that?"

"The centre of the case has moved into this hemisphere."

"Don't I know it."

"Coming on the same plane as Limm and the girl?" inquired Shaw.

"I'll let you know," said Roger. "I very much doubt it."

Hardy was in early that Friday. It was one of his good mornings—Roger sometimes wondered whether his moods were due to pressures at home.

"It's taken you a long time to get round to it," he said. "Yes—the same plane as Limm is a good idea. Can Kebble keep your office ticking over?"

In a curious mood between excitement and apprehension, Roger said:

"He's certainly worth a trial. Then I'll go?"

"Don't ask me to square it with your wife," Hardy said drily.

13

FLIGHT

JANET was at London Airport to see Roger off. Both boys had staked a claim to accompany her, but they were at their jobs, and Janet, trying not to show how much she wished she was going, was allowed into the roped-off section where the passengers waited. This was almost the identical spot where Percy Sheldon had died. Over by that same buffet, open to passengers and visitors and doing a brisk trade, Paul Barring *alias* Jessup had jabbed home the deadly needle.

Limm was standing there with Doreen.

In another corner Cyril Gee and his Sal were present under restrained protest, to tell the police if they saw anyone who had been here on the afternoon of Sheldon's death. So far they had shown no sign. It was just on ten o'clock, and the call for the passengers to board the aircraft would soon be made. Janet was almost too bright-eyed; Australia was a long way off, and Roger's trips abroad too few for her to be used to saying good-bye for any long period.

"... and if it's too hot in Sydney, you must buy a light-weight suit," she was saying.

That was when young Cyril Gee seemed to come alive. He had seen someone he recognized. Roger moved his head to look about. Janet went on talking. Gee was looking towards a noisy group near the news-stand. Two policemen, including Sandys of the airport police, were watching him. The members of the party moved, hilariously, and beyond them Roger could now see Lancelot Smith, the *Blue Flag Line*'s London manager.

Gee caught Roger's eye.

"You haven't heard a word I've said," Janet said, more forlorn than angry. "Roger, *please*. It's a different climate, and it's bound to take you a day or two to get used to it. You must be careful."

A clear voice sounded above hers, above all the sounds of the airport building.

"*Will all passengers for Flight 34 for Zürich, Rome, Beirut, Bahrain, Delhi, Bangkok, Hong Kong, and Sydney please take their seats.*"

There was a surge forward by thirty or forty passengers, those eager to move off. The crowd was suddenly much thinner. Lancelot Smith, his simian face strangely incongruous against his immaculate clothes, drew nearer the cordon. He was looking about him as if in desperation—as if he must see someone he knew to be here but was afraid he was too late.

He saw Roger, and changed direction. So did Sandys, and a Yard man, but they were farther away. Roger felt a moment of absolute panic. It was as if Smith was coming at him, with murder in his eyes. He carried an umbrella and raised it. Janet said in sudden alarm:

"Roger! What is it?"

Roger stepped swiftly in front of her, as if that umbrella was lethal.

"Mr. West!" called Smith. "Mr. West." He was waving his umbrella.

"This is ridiculous," Roger thought. "He can't mean any harm, I'm making a fool of myself."

"*Roger!*" breathed Janet.

"*Mr. West!* Superintendent——"

Sandys and the big Yard man ranged themselves on either side of Smith; even if he intended harm he could do none now. Roger raised one hand to acknowledge him, and touched Janet's shoulder.

"Just stay here. I won't be a minute." He went forward. Neither of the other detectives touched Smith but they were within hands' reach. He did not seem to notice them. His upper lip was beaded with big blobs of perspiration. His thick, ponderous lower lip was quivering. His eyes seemed buried behind the high cheekbones.

"Mr. West, there is something I must tell you."

Janet was whispering in Roger's ear.

"Jan, quiet, *please*. Yes, Mr. Smith?" His voice changed from imploring to curt and hostile. Smith was only a foot or two away from him. He was breathing heavily; stertorously. His words came out with great difficulty.

"I want to warn—to warn—you. It could happen to—to any ship of ours. Any ship. Believe me. None is safe." Sweat in great blobs was on his forehead. "I should have told you before. I was too—too frightened."

Janet was whispering.

"For God's sake keep quiet!" Roger half turned as he spoke to her, and saw how shocked she was. The Yard man by Smith had his notebook out. "Who is doing this?" Roger demanded roughly. "Where is——"

Smith staggered. Sandys grabbed him, as if afraid he would fall.

"*He's terribly ill!*" Janet cried.

That was what she had been trying to say.

"Find the—the Barring family. They—they hate——"
Smith choked on the word, then sucked in a rasping breath.

"Where is Solomon Barring?" Roger asked, now almost
savagely. "Is there anyone else? Tell me!"

"Marcus—Marcus is back in Australia. I don't—don't
know where Solomon is. I don't——"

Smith almost fell, his knees buckling, out of control.

"*He's dying,*" Janet cried. "Get a doctor! Roger, get a
doctor."

Smith looked like a great ape as he clutched Sandys' arm.

"I took—I took strychnine," he gasped. "I couldn't face—
face my responsibility. I should have told——"

A man pushed his way through the crowd as Smith broke
into a piercing scream of agony. He fell out of Sandys' grasp,
his body seemed to writhe, then straightened out as if he were
on a rack; then arched. The thrusting man bent over him as
he screamed again but it was only a rasping echo of the earlier
sound.

Roger stood staring, Janet beside him, shocked.

"*Will all passengers for Flight 34 for Zürich, Rome, Beirut,
Bahrain, Delhi, Bangkok, Hong Kong, and Sydney please take
their seats.*"

Sandys said gruffly: "I'll get that flight postponed for half
an hour." He moved off as other policemen came up.

Near by the Gees stood, stunned as was everyone who had
seen or heard, staring at the stricken man. Roger was acutely
conscious of the way he had shouted at Janet, yet was trying to
assimilate all that Smith had told him. Now he knew more of
the truth and the full horror of what could happen, it tore at
his mind.

Janet stood in front of him.

"It's all right, darling," she said. "Don't worry about me,
please don't worry." She was pleading. "It was my fault."

"*Your*——"

"I'm going to leave, you must look after this," Janet said.

Her eyes were glistening with tears, her hand was tight on his. "Take care of yourself." She put her face up.

He bent down, slowly. Suddenly, he swept her into his arms, and held her close with a fierce hug. He could feel her heart thumping, thumping. He could feel his heart, racing, racing. How much she meant to him; how much they meant to each other.

He let her go. He had a glimpse of her face for a moment; it was radiant. Then she turned and pushed her way through the crowd. The cordon was gone, so many police and officials were about. Smith had come out of the first spasm, and his body was relaxed, but the next would come soon, bringing its agony; and the next and the next, until he died.

Could the doctor help him?

He was trying to say something as he lay there, looking at Roger. Roger moved forward, and went down on one knee. Smith was whispering:

"Did this—myself. Awful—awful—quite awful. Save— save them. Please save——"

Then his body was caught in the awful second spasm, the breath was forced out of his mouth in a hideous screech, his body arched. The doctor said to Roger:

"We'll have him away in a few seconds. I doubt if he'll talk again."

"Can you help him?"

"With the pain, yes. He's gone too far for anything else."

"Will passengers for Flight 34 to Zürich, Rome, and places East please take their seats."

Two men appeared with a stretcher, and Sandys arrived just as they were lifting Smith on to it.

"Take your time, Handsome—you can have twenty minutes. If you decide to catch a later plane——"

Doreen Morrison and Ben Limm were on this one.

"I'll catch 34," Roger said. "I'll just have a word with my chaps." He moved, and saw Kebble, hurrying. The incredible thing about the young sergeant was that whenever he was wanted he was at hand. "What's brought you?" Roger demanded.

"Smith rang up and said he had to talk to you," Kebble answered. "He sounded desperate, so I thought I ought to be here if he missed you." Kebble looked at the stretcher and the now relaxed figure covered with a blanket. "Did he say anything?"

Roger told him.

"My God!" Kebble muttered. "And there are twenty-seven ships in that line."

"Telephone Sydney, talk to Shaw, tell him exactly what Smith said," ordered Roger. "Don't make any suggestion about what to do—leave it entirely to him. The sergeant here made a lot of notes—give Shaw the lot, won't you?"

"Yes, sir."

"Keep my wife posted," Roger said. "She saw the collapse, but she may not believe Smith committed suicide. Check, make sure—I don't think there's any doubt, but make sure— then call on my wife and tell her. Otherwise she'll run around with the idea that it will be my turn next."

"I'll tell her," Kebble promised.

Roger shook hands.

"Take a night off now and again, for Kitty's sake," he said. "Never lose a chance of time off, Keb—there'll be a hell of a lot of nights when you'll have to stand her up."

Kebble looked astounded. "You know about *Kit*?"

Roger grinned.

"The Yard's just a big village," he said. "You'll find out."

He turned and made his way to the entrance gate, stepped through to the vast expanse of the airfield. He was almost deafened by the roar of a great plane, some distance off. He had expected to see a Comet; instead a Boeing 707 was waiting. Officials hurried with him through the drizzle sweeping miserably across the airfield, even the waiting fire-trucks and petrol-tenders looked forlorn, and a few mechanics were huddled up in macintoshes against the rain.

"The first-class door is shut, sir, you won't mind walking through the economy class, will you?"

"I thought that's where I was booked."

"We like to look after our top Yard man, sir!"

Roger smiled. "Nice of you." But he wouldn't be so close to Limm. He climbed up into the aircraft, where two stewards and a stewardess were waiting for him. The stewardess led the way towards the front.

"Just follow me, sir."

He knew that the passengers were staring at him. A man said in an audible whisper: "Some people never learn to be on time." Limm, on the outside seat next to Doreen, seemed about to speak, but did not. Doreen's knees were pressed close together; for some odd reason Roger remembered her rather big calves. The stewardess led the way through an open door, into a cabin which was much more spacious, and with larger seats, two on each side of the gangway.

There were two empty seats on the right.

"Here you are, Mr. West. Seat 7." The girl smiled. She was not particularly pretty, but had a nice smile and was beauti- fully made up. "Fasten your seat belt right away, please."

"About time, too," a woman remarked sourly.

She didn't matter. Nothing mattered but the fate of hun- dreds, thousands of people, sailing the seven seas in Blue Flag Line ships. A picture of Smith's ugly, almost animal-like face hovered in front of Roger's mind. Not daring to face up to the responsibility, the manager had preferred to kill himself. How much more could he have told? Conceivably enough to make a quick end to this case.

Why hadn't he wanted to stay alive?

The aircraft was taxi-ing. Behind Roger, a woman said: "This is always the moment I hate most." There was a fierce roar and rush of noise, a sense of surging motion. Aircraft, buildings, green fields, and motor-cars seemed to rush by. There was a curious kind of silent commotion, a feeling of tension and at the same time of relaxation. The smiling stewardess stood by the lounge door, and a steward talked in a cheerful faintly Cockney voice farther along. The clouds were thick grey-white mist groping at the windows.

Suddenly, there was bright, almost blinding light; the sun, shining on top of clouds which lost their greyness and were soft and billowing white. Above, the sky was unbelievably blue.

Roger settled back in his seat.

Smith's face faded from his mind's eye; Janet's, touched with that radiance, replaced it. Why the devil had he let fly at her like that? He knew the answer, even though it failed to satisfy him. He was far too tense and worked up about this case, with a sense of deep personal involvement. It was no use arguing that the case warranted such tension, anyhow. A policeman must be objective, free from emotional reactions, one could not see the whole of the problem until he did. In a way the flight should help him. He could relax for forty-eight hours, doze, sleep, eat, drink, let the facts drift through his mind. If he needed to send messages, he could do so over the radio; if any news came for him he would have it almost as quickly as he would on the telephone in his office.

The Channel was hidden by thick cloud. There being nothing to see, Roger closed his eyes. He seemed to have been sitting there for ten minutes when the stewardess touched his shoulder.

"Fasten your seat belt, please."

"Already? Why?" Roger struggled up.

"We're approaching Zürich, Mr. West."

"That's the quickest hour I've ever passed," Roger said ruefully.

"We made up some time, the wind was behind us," the stewardess told him. "We have three-quarters of an hour here, sir. Will you leave the plane?"

"I think so," Roger said.

As they lost height he got a confused impression of a big city and a big expanse of blue water, all beautiful in the sunlight; London's drizzle seemed a thousand miles away. Of course, it almost was! He saw one group of people streaming towards customs, and others waiting about. He left his coat inside the cabin and stepped into summer warmth. A car drew up alongside him and a good-looking, middle-aged man got out.

"I believe you are Superintendent West."

"That's right." Roger sounded as surprised as he felt.

"I am Inspector Müller," the other said, and shook hands. "I am sorry your visit to Zürich is so brief, but from Kloten here we have a half-hour's drive to the city, so it is too far. You will have a drink, though, I hope."

"I'd be happy to," Roger said appreciatively.

"Please get in." Müller was as immaculate as Smith had been. He closed the door, settled down, and said in a different tone: "I have a message for you, Superintendent. The man Lancelot Smith is dead. That is bad news, I fear."

Depression swept Roger's good spirits away.

I wonder if we'll ever know how bad, he thought.

Brooding over the case could not stop Roger from being transfixed by the beauty and the grandeur of the Alps. He sensed how all passengers were enthralled as they glided over the thrusting, glistening peaks, the almost audible sigh of regret when they passed over the foothills and flew over the plains. The Mediterranean appeared, so rich a blue that it looked unreal. The ships on it were like white toys. Roger approached Rome, half apprehensive in case there should be another message. There was none, but two handsome Roman police officials were there to greet him with news that the Donellis appeared to be happy and in no danger at Naples.

"We shall look after them, there is nothing to worry about," one man said confidently.

Limm and Doreen also stretched their legs. They kept close together, as young lovers might.

No one met him at Beirut.

Immediately after dinner they flew into a moonless sky in which the stars seemed to scatter themselves about the aircraft. Roger slept, dreamlessly. He stayed in his seat at Bahrain and slept again to Delhi. As he stepped out of the aircraft there into a cool early morning with the dawn glowing faintly beyond the horizon, a Sikh in western clothes but wearing a huge turban, came forward, teeth dazzling white against his great black beard.

"Roger, my good friend!"

"Ram Singh!" Roger's heart leapt. Only six months ago this Indian detective had stayed for a month in London, spending much time with Roger both at the Yard and at home.

"It is wicked for you to have so little time, I cannot even arrange a rope-trick for you! I have a message, though, from your office."

Roger's heart lurched.

"Is it good news or bad?"

"It is to tell you that a Mr. Samuel Hackett—*Hackett* is right, yes?—has been located in France. He appears to be in excellent health. Also," went on Ram Singh, "a message from Sydney, Australia, comes from Superintendent Shaw. I met him when he flew through Delhi three years ago. He says you cannot arrive at Sydney soon enough for him. He has been informed about the warning from a man named Smith. He says also that he takes the case very seriously indeed."

The big Sikh was no longer smiling; it was as if he were touched by anxiety just as much as Roger. As they stood there, Ben Limm and Doreen came out of the other exit of the aircraft. The girl looked very tired, and even Limm's vitality seemed to have wilted. Roger waved, the others waved back, the Sikh said:

"Obviously you take it very seriously, too."

14

HONG KONG WELCOME

"The captain's compliments, Mr. West, and would you like to go up front with him as we approach Hong Kong?" The second officer, a tall, amiable-looking young man with a broken nose, bent over Roger. "We'll be there in twenty-five minutes."

"I'd like to very much," Roger said.

Several of the passengers who had come all the way from London watched, but no longer with any sign of envy; everyone now knew who he was, and the familiar, often welcome but sometimes exasperating sense of awe of a senior policeman showed clearly. He went through the lounge, where three men and one middle-aged woman dressed like a teenager were drinking, then stepped on to the flight deck. There was more noise, some vibration, and an appearance of high organization and efficiency. Ahead was the instrument panel, so big and complicated that it seemed to need a man with a robot mind to understand it.

The second pilot's seat was empty. The captain turned, beckoned, leaned across, and shook hands as Roger settled into the seat.

"Sorry we haven't had a chance to meet before, Superintendent."

"I'm glad of it now," Roger said.

"Proud to have you with us."

Roger murmured a disclaimer.

"I'm just a policeman."

The captain smiled.

"I've heard you called other things." He turned away. "How about *that,* sir? Red China and Hong Kong, looking thick as thieves."

Ahead was a mass of land beyond a sea which was as blue as the Mediterranean. The great rocks of Hong Kong and the surrounding islands looked like huge diamonds as they glistened in the sun. The water was dotted with small craft and large; liners, cargo boats, sampans, countless junks with dark-brown sails. As they drew nearer, Roger could pick out spots he had often seen in pictures but never in real life.

"We fly low over Victoria, the city on Hong Kong Island," the captain said. "Famous for its shanty towns and the homes in the rocks, or William Holden and Suzie Wong, whichever you prefer. Over there is Kowloon, you see where the long isthmus strikes out—there's a plane taking off."

Roger said: "I see it. It's surpassed all my expectations already."

"First time?"

"Yes."

"Just sit back and take it in," said the captain. "I won't spoil it with chatter. If you want to know anything——"

"Those white boats—I can see four or five of them," Roger said.

"Ferries from Hong Kong to Kowloon."

"Oh."

"Wonderful organization, and always has been." After a few moments' silence while Roger marvelled, the captain asked: "Spending any time here?"

"Just a few hours. Do you fly the plane on to Darwin and Sydney?"

"Not this one. I may do tomorrow's flight, I don't know who it will be today, I'm afraid. If you can spare any of your couple of hours to look round the place, jump at the chance. I go round every month or so and still don't believe it. See you before I go off, sir."

"Good," Roger said. "Thanks."

He was about to get up, and the island seemed very close, crowded with houses and people, when he saw a ship with a white funnel and a blue flag on it. The sight of it was like a physical blow. Both captain and second pilot looked at him curiously. As he went back to his seat, he no longer saw the islands and the water as places of grandeur, but as the place where the *Kookaburra* had called only a week or ten days earlier, where nearly all the Blue Flag Line ships called. At his window he looked out, trying to spot the ship again.

There it was, by itself at a quay which jutted out from the mainland. Near it was a railway.

"Fasten your belts, please," came over the loudspeaker.

The water seemed to be coming up to engulf them until suddenly they bumped, bounced, then ran along the tarmac with the blue waters stretching out on either side. The stewardess came up to Roger.

"There's a messenger waiting for you, Mr. West. Hope you enjoy the rest of the trip."

"I will if it's like this one." Roger shook hands.

He was the first out into the gilded sunlight of the late afternoon. At the foot of the steps, even before they were pushed properly into position, was a tall, smiling man—Luke Shaw of the Sydney C.I.B. with another tall, leaner man— Fred Hodges of the Hong Kong police.

They gripped hands, equally pleased to see one another, and moved off together towards a police car, until Roger said suddenly:

"You two will have my stripes. Limm and Doreen Morrison are on board, I don't want them to wander off on their own."

"I've three men here who've studied their photographs," Hodges said comfortingly. "Can't you slacken off even for an hour?"

"If I get the chance."

"I've told Luke that you can forget the *Kookaburra* while you're here," said Hodges. "He can brief you on the way to Sydney—he's learned all there is to see here."

"Don't tell Handsome West that," protested Shaw. "He'll want to check for himself." They were getting into the car. "I arrived yesterday, Handsome, to check all I could with the agents of the Blue Flag Line here. It's the second most important office. The head office is in Sydney, but you knew that."

"Didn't stop him from doing the Hong Kong Island trip— *and* the night clubs. What an appetite for legs these Aussies have." Hodges laughed heartily. "We can fit in——"

He stopped abruptly, looking across the airfield, snapped: "Swing round, Ling," to the Chinese chauffeur, and added almost in the same breath: "I've just seen the nastiest piece of work in Kowloon, proper artist with a knife." To the chauffeur he barked: "That cyclist—catch him."

The cyclist was a hundred yards away, near the airport buildings. Two cars and a fire-truck were in the way of the police car. Roger felt a desperate desire to get out and run towards the passengers now moving from the airport building towards coaches marked: *'Special Tours'*. The cyclist was nearer those than the police car when Ben Limm and Doreen appeared.

"Honk your horn!" roared Hodges.

The driver swung round the last car, hand on horn, blaring. All the passengers and officials started, looked round and stared. The cyclist was heading straight for Limm and Doreen. Roger felt a thousand miles away, and utterly helpless.

Limm sprang in front of the girl as the cyclist drew up. Even from this distance, Roger saw a flash, as of steel. Then two men near Limm and the girl flung themselves at the cyclist. There was a fierce, vicious struggle, a human dog-fight. One man backed away, blood streaming from a nasty cut in his left hand. As the car pulled up, the cyclist went down with a thud, his head banged on the hard ground, and the knife clattered from his hand.

Hodges was breathing hard.

"I told you we'd look after her," he said.

Doreen Morrison was huddled against Limm, her head on his chest. His long arms were about her, protectingly. He was staring down at the assailant and the bloodstained knife, horror reflected in his eyes.

Roger found himself speaking.

"Who did he come for, Limm? You or Doreen?"

Limm didn't speak.

"He went for the girl, no doubt about that," said the policeman. "If he'd wanted the man he could have got him with a single throw."

"The man saved her," another policeman chimed in.

"That made him pretty quick," Hodges remarked.

"Almost as if he knew what was coming." Luke Shaw was looking so intently at Limm that Limm turned his head and stared at him, without moving his arms from the girl. "That's Benjamin Limm, isn't it?"

"Yes," answered Roger.

"If he knew what was going to happen, why should he save her life?" asked Hodges.

"We need to know a lot more about Ben Limm," said Shaw heavily. "You weren't slow on the up-take, Fred. Say you know the Chinaman?"

"Yes, I know Wu Hong," Hodges said. He watched as the assailant was pulled to his feet and handcuffed. He raised his voice: "Take him to my office, I'll be along." To Roger and Shaw he continued: "He's Wu Hong, once one of the trouble-shooters for a big tong, until it went respectable. He's what they call an artist with a knife—he can hit a moving target at thirty yards and a motionless one at fifty. He had to come close to avoid the people round her. Otherwise she'd be dead. Let's get going."

"I'll have a word with Ben Limm, and make sure the girl's guarded, Fred," Roger said to Hodges. He moved across as the girl eased herself from the big Australian. Her eyes looked huge and her face so white she looked as if she would faint. "Is she all right?"

"Just about," Limm grunted.

"Thanks to you," Roger said.

"I did the only thing."

"How well do you know Wu Hong?"

Limm's eyes narrowed as if in surprise.

"Who?"

"The attacker."

"What the hell are you trying to say?" Limm demanded angrily. "I saw him take his knife out—I'd been watching for anything suspicious. You told me she would be in danger, didn't you?"

"I warned you," Roger said. "From now on she will be under close police protection—while here in Hong Kong, on the aircraft, and in Sydney."

"Who's objecting?" Limm was more his truculent than his angry self now.

Doreen must have understood every word, but she showed no sign. She reminded Roger vividly of the way she had looked in the room at Notting Hill, when she had been so near death. Looking at her he felt he could almost feel something of her anguish. Soon, questions so obvious that they were easy to overlook, came to his mind.

Why should anyone be so determined to kill her? Surely she *must* know the answer to that at least.

And why was Limm never attacked?

Roger went back to the car and got in. The chauffeur closed the door on him and hurried to the wheel. Hodges, in front, was turning round and talking to Shaw. As the car moved off, Hodges said:

"We can take care of this, Handsome. No need for you to miss your sightseeing."

"The only sight I want to see is Fred's office, and Wu Hong's face when he starts talking," Roger said.

15

WU HONG

IT was easy to have preconceived notions about people, dangerously easy to generalize. The Chinese were said so often to be inscrutable. Wu Hong was a little, wizened man with skin like old parchment, eyes bloodshot, hands full of dark-blue veins. He wore a faded blue denim shirt and khaki trousers so often washed that they seemed no colour at all. In his nervousness he smiled widely at the policemen, showing gaps in his yellow teeth.

"He's full to the neck with opium," Hodges said. "Lives on the damned stuff." He stood up from his big desk as Wu Hong came slowly in. He didn't speak to the Chinaman for a long time, just stared at him. The smile became a grin, the eyes puckered, the almost colourless lips quivered.

Hodges spoke suddenly, softly, in Chinese. His manner was almost friendly. Wu Hong answered in a spate of words, clack, clack, clack, clack, clack. Hodges interrupted, there was a sharp exchange, and then the Chinaman averted his eyes.

Hodges said in English:

"Marcus Barring hired him for the job."

"*Marcus Barring,*" ejaculated Shaw. "Did he come through here?"

"Yes—so Wu Hong says. Five days ago."

"But he couldn't have known then that Doreen Morrison was coming this way or on this plane," objected Roger sharply.

"He said she would probably be coming through, and Wu Hong was to watch each aircraft for the girl. Barring showed him a photograph of her, so that he could recognize her."

"But *this* plane," Shaw said sceptically.

"Don't make a mystery of it," Hodges protested. "Wu Hong knows a dozen people who work at the airport. There aren't so many aircraft flying in here, all he had to do was be near by so that he could pick up a message from anyone on the airport staff who knew when planes were due. Ten minutes' notice was all he needed, on his bike. We'll start inquiries to try to find out who tipped him off, but it won't be easy."

"I'd like a go at him now," Luke Shaw said firmly.

Hodges grinned.

"You'd be welcome—he'd have the time of his life lying to you in pidgin English."

"Fred," Roger said, "how much did Barring pay him?"

"Two hundred Hong Kong dollars. Say twelve pounds ten."

"To *kill*?"

"Life's cheap here," Hodges said drily. "Too cheap."

"Has he worked for Barring before?"

"I'll try him with that one," Hodges said.

"Try him by saying you know he killed Neil Sanderson, of the *Kookaburra*," Roger suggested.

"Don't get me wrong, but it might take weeks to get a full story out of this man," Hodges said. "We're damned lucky he named Marcus Barring so early. He probably knows Barring is on the run already. He can't deny the attack on the Morrison girl, but he can deny knowing anything about the murder of Sanderson. I might be able to break him down but I'd have to use all the tricks the Chinese know, and it can't be done in a hurry."

When Hodges stopped, Roger said briefly: "Sorry I spoke."

"I mean it, Handsome. No offence intended."

Roger grinned. "Don't be an idiot, of course there wasn't."

"Tell you what," put in Luke Shaw, who never liked to keep silent for long, "now you've got a start, Fred, keep at Wu Hong and his tong friends, and give the Blue Flag Line all you've got. We'll keep in touch by radio-telephone if needs be."

"Fair enough," agreed Hodges. He nodded to the men who were guarding the Chinaman. "Take him away. Don't let him get near any stuff, he might crack sooner than we expect if he has to go without it."

"Stuff?" echoed Shaw.

"Opium."

"You talk as if it were as easy to get as aspirin."

"That's how they can get the crude stuff out here," Hodges said. "We have all our work cut out to stop them refining it and exporting it to the U.S.A. Next time you're this way remind us to tell you all about the opium business." He grinned as he looked at his watch. "We could delay that aircraft, Handsome."

"Let's get off on time," Roger urged. "The quicker we're in Australia the better."

"You're learning." Shaw grinned.

"Come back with your wife another time, I'll lay everything on," Hodges said earnestly. "Damned sorry you couldn't look around this time. But you've one treat in store. Hong Kong by night from the air is fantastic."

Roger leaned against his window and stared at the stars below him; or lights which looked like stars of a hundred different colours. Lights glimmered and shimmered from ships and ferries and reflected in the water. Lights blazed from the city of Kowloon. Lights of cars streaked about the mainland and curved about the steep roads of the island like shooting stars seen in a mirror. For the first time since the attack on Doreen, Roger forgot the case.

For the first time since then, too, Doreen relaxed. She stared down at the fairyland, enthralled, and said in a low-pitched voice:

"Isn't it wonderful, Ben?"

"Wonderful," Limm echoed huskily.

As they gained height, she leaned against him. His right arm slid round her waist, and was still. She looked up into his eyes, without speaking. He raised his hand, very slowly, to the gentle swell of her breast, and she smiled, and nestled closer.

Soon, she said: "Ben, you'll always keep me safe, won't you?"

"I'll keep you safe," he promised.

On the deck of the S.S. *Kookaburra*, now sailing past the southern tip of the Isle of Celebes towards the Timor Sea at a steady sixteen knots, Jack and Jill Parrish were standing at the rail. The night was starlit and calm, and very warm. Jill wore a thin cotton frock, a bra, and panties; all the night demanded. Jack Parrish, twelve years or so her senior, stood with his arms about her, caressingly. It was as if it was impossible for them to be alone together too often. Each was completely absorbed in the other.

Their cheeks touched.

"There's only one thing wrong," Jill said softly.

"Nothing's wrong, my sweet."

"We've six days left, that's all."

"We've a lifetime left," Jack Parrish said.

"It can't ever be *quite* the same."

"You'd be surprised how romantic banana plantations can be," Parrish said, and made her laugh. That was one of the wonderful things about him: he could always make her laugh, always make her relish every minute of living.

A passenger, a man, walked past them, cigarette glowing.

"Goodnight."

They echoed: "Goodnight." Parrish squeezed his wife's waist again, and said: "We might as well go down."

"Hm—hm."

She stood and watched the dark bosom of the sea, until he led her slowly, gently, to their cabin.

Old Sam Hackett lay in bed.

He knew by now that he wasn't so young as he once had been, and he was tired—nearly exhausted. He was also very,

very contented! It was a strange feeling for a man who had been so active most of his life, and never content when doing nothing.

He watched Thérèse.

She was thirty-five or six, he knew, and that was very young to him. He had admired her fine figure from the time they had first met, when he had been on a night-club tour of Paris and she had been a hostess. Now he could admire her body, so full, so firm. She was not shameless, but simply natural with him.

He could ask her to marry him.

He could not make up his mind whether to or not, for two reasons. She might refuse, and that would be a great blow to his pride, for he believed she loved him. It had been a strange belief at first, but now it was firm and deep, although he was afraid to put it to the test. The second reason was one he resented in a way, although he could blame only himself for it.

Did he really *want* to get married? A widower for over ten years, he had been used to doing exactly what he pleased and going wherever he wished. Just now, this Junoesque woman with her broken English and her matter-of-factness, infatuated him. He wanted nothing more than to be with her. She turned away from the table, where she had been making coffee with an electric percolator. She wore a short-length dressing-gown, open at the front, and it gaped farther as she carried two full cups nearly at arms' length. She sat down in a wicker chair filled with cushions, balancing the cups dexterously.

She handed him one.

"This is what you need, old one," she said. Her eyes laughed at him. "This will make a man of you!"

He found himself laughing.

What *would* she say if he asked her to marry him? Would she laugh at him, then? Did she know how rich he was? What would his friends say if he took a new wife back to Australia?

As the 707 flew towards Sydney the sky in the east was a glory in gold touched with red, rich as a deep rose lit by the bright morning sun. The light spread over the sleeping city, lighting up the windows of the tall, new skyscrapers, bathing the clear, calm water of the harbour with its warm beauty. The beaches, surf-rimmed as if with sugar icing, stretched in all directions. The bridge was like an enormous toy, and already busy with traffic.

"Our new headquarters is over there," Luke Shaw said, pointing. "We haven't moved in yet. And even then we won't have everything in the same building. Funny thing, they'll spend millions on business houses and opera houses but when it comes to police headquarters we have to settle for an old factory. The tall, narrow building; the new one with the silvery look, that's Ocean House. The Blue Flag Line's offices are on the top two floors. The directors and their secretaries are on the top floor—fourteen. I told you that Raymond Flag is the chairman and I told you that his brother Gregory is the managing director, didn't I? They're both Australian born."

"And Mortimer, the secretary, is an English cousin who's been here fifteen years," Roger said. "Yes, you told me."

"Thought you might have forgotten," Luke said slyly. Then more excitedly: "Look down there! See, near the docks—follow the harbour along from the bridge, see that ship? Is she moving in or out?"

Roger craned his neck forward to see, and immediately saw the white funnel and the blue flag painted on it. Then it was lost to sight as the aircraft made a slow turn.

"There's our problem," Shaw went on. "Whether to warn all the masters of the ships or not. I told you I think we should, and I've told the Commissioner, too. We're due for that conference this afternoon. We'll have the answer then."

"What does the Commissioner think?" asked Roger.

"Don't know. He's a fly old customer, you can never be sure which way he'll jump—but he won't be difficult at the conference, if he decides against us he'll tell us ourselves."

Roger, watching the green fields of the Kingsford Smith Airport, didn't speak.

"I'm taking it for granted you think everyone should be warned," Shaw said. "You haven't said so yet, Handsome."

"Haven't sized it up in my mind," Roger admitted. "Let's see what turns up." He saw the notice to fasten seat belts flash on and off; it was becoming almost second nature to do so now. A plumper, prettier stewardess went along to check the belts. The aircraft lost height. He wondered how Doreen Morrison was feeling, felt that sense of impending disaster as he had so often. He was on his feet almost as soon as they had come to a standstill, and the first out of the cabin. The sun was blinding, almost white. He climbed down the steps with Shaw on his heels. A police car was waiting, and several plain-clothes men were standing about.

"Three of my chaps are there to look after the girl and Limm," said Shaw. "You worry too much. Nothing will happen here."

Roger didn't speak.

Soon, Limm and Doreen got down. The girl was nervous, glancing about her in all directions. If danger struck, she seemed to say, this was when it would strike hardest; and that was probably true. C.I.B. men ranged themselves alongside the couple. Limm kept his arm round Doreen, even when they were close to a police car.

"They're all right," Shaw said with satisfaction as they got in. "What about coming to my place for a bit of breakfast, Handsome?"

"Luke, do you know what I'd like to do?"

Shaw grinned.

"Be on your own for a few hours, hey?"

"I might get rid of these nerves you say I've got."

"Okay, okay. There'll be plenty of time to meet my better half. You've got a reservation at the Wentworth, it's the quietest of our big hotels. Soon going to be pulled down," he added. "There won't be any of old Sydney left, soon."

The police car with Doreen and Limm turned out of the airport.

"In half an hour they'll be tucked up in a small hotel, which will be guarded back and front," said Shaw. "No one else knows which hotel, so there can't be a reception party."

Roger said quietly: "Luke, so far they've managed to kill anyone they've set their minds on. We don't really know why, we don't know who's next on their list, if anyone. Until we've caught the two Barring brothers and we know the danger's over, I'm not going to rest easy. Are you?"

Shaw grinned.

"Maybe I'm harder-hearted than you," he said. "Maybe that's why I think every Blue Flag Line ship should be warned of danger—every Master compelled to have his vessel searched. We don't *know* that the *Koala* was blown up, we don't *know* that the *Kookaburra* will be—but the risk is great enough for action stations for my money. That's what I'm going to fight for at the conference."

Roger nodded.

"Try to see it my way," Shaw urged. "There are some papers in your room giving you a break-down on the Blue Flag Line and the men who run it. They'll all be at the conference, and if you think I'm a hard nut, you wait until you meet them."

The room at the hotel overlooked a small, triangular green, and by craning his neck Roger could just see the top of the great arch of the bridge. After a shower and breakfast, he settled down to the documents, and was halfway through them when his telephone rang.

"Handsome, that conference has been put off until to-morrow," Luke Shaw said. "There's a big company fraud brewing up and I've got to spend time on it. Mortimer Flag's flown to Adelaide about some trouble with a cargo of hides. Like a man to show you round?"

"Let me find my own way," Roger said.

"I can easily send a man——"

"I'd like to get the feel of this place," Roger said, and meant it.

He spent much of the day walking, and took an occasional bus ride, using a map from the hotel. He went to the tall, silvery-walled Ocean House where the Blue Flag Line had its headquarters, the wharves, the Bridge lookout, the small private hotel where Limm and Doreen were staying. All the time he felt a sense of urgency conflicting with a desire to see more and more of the city.

That night he had dinner at Luke Shaw's home near Manly, a small white house on a hill overlooking a small bay. Mrs. Shaw, small, unexpectedly young looking and bright-eyed, cooked leg of lamb to rare succulence.

"I know you haven't done much today," Luke said. "But you'll benefit from it, Handsome. Any new ideas during the day?"

"They're simmering," Roger said, and added under his breath: "I hope."

Next morning he stood looking at the triangle of green grass and shrubs, and farther away, the sweeping approaches to the Harbour Bridge; from here the bridge looked more man-made, more as if it belonged to the surroundings. He brooded for five minutes, then had a shower and ordered breakfast. He went back to the window, half wishing he could see a Blue Flag steamer.

He noticed a man strolling across the green, one of several who had been lounging and lazing there, night workers or layabouts. Roger moved away, then looked from one side of the window; the man was moving nearer, glancing towards the hotel. Roger felt his pulse racing. At this distance he couldn't be sure, but this looked like Marcus Barring. He went to his bag, took out a small pair of field-glasses, and reached the window again when there was a knock at the door.

"Come in!"

He focused the glasses on the man on the green as an elderly waiter came in with a tray.

Marcus Barring was, indeed, watching the hotel. There was now no doubt of his rather heavy features, the glasses even showed his pitted face.

Between grapefruit, bacon and eggs, toast and marmalade Roger kept looking out. Barring was still lounging, keeping to himself although more men were about now. Roger finished, deliberated, and decided not to call Shaw. Every now and again a chance had to be taken, and he decided to take one now. He opened the box again, put the glasses away, and took out a small, whippy cosh, the only weapon he carried wherever he went. He put this in his jacket pocket, and went downstairs and outside. He strolled towards the Harbour Bridge, held up at the main road by the flow of morning rush-hour traffic. When he was safely across he strolled as far as he could towards the bridge, then turned back. Already his exploration of the city the day before was proving invaluable.

Barring was now across the road.

Roger strolled farther along, looking at the street map. There was a criss-cross of narrow streets, some leading down towards the river. He did not look round except at one corner, a deliberate appraisal of the old terraced houses and the trees. Barring was still behind him, dressed in pale-grey trousers and a loose-fitting sweater. Then he went on, along Kent Street, crossed several other turnings. It was summer warmth for him, already; he wished he could take his jacket off. He saw the masts and funnels of shipping down another side street, and walked to a bridge from which he could see a great stretch of the harbour. There were thirty or forty vessels in sight, and two of them had Blue Flag funnels. He went down a flight of stone steps towards the river but even on a small jetty jutting out into the water, he could not get near enough to see them clearly.

"I wonder if Luke's watching them." He half regretted his decision not to call the Sydney man.

He told himself there was no need to wonder, that Luke Shaw was not a man to leave anything to chance. He actually smiled. Luke would pull out all the stops to show the Yard what Sydney could do.

Still smiling, Roger turned.

The man who had tried to knife Doreen Morrison in London was only ten yards behind him, right hand in his pocket, as if he held a knife.

16

BRAGGART?

"SUPERINTENDENT BLOODY WEST," Barring rasped. "You didn't expect to see me, cobber, did you?"

Roger said equably: "I hoped to, Barring."

"Don't give me that."

"I hoped to," Roger repeated. "From the moment I saw you from my window. Who told you I was at the Wentworth?"

"The birds," jeered Barring. "They'll take Shaw the news of your death, too."

"Not for a long, long time," Roger said. He put his hand to his jacket pocket; Barring watched very closely. He took out a packet of cigarettes, and some matches, lit up, and put cigarettes and matches back. He felt the smooth leather of the cosh, curled round inside. "Let me tell you something. Wu Hong told us all about your generous payment for a murder which didn't come off. If you want hirelings to do their job properly, you ought to pay them better. You get paid enough."

"And I'll get a bonus for killing you." Barring kept his hand in his pocket; he seemed to clench it there.

"Kill me, and you'll have every policeman in Australia and England looking for you," Roger said. "You're in a bad enough jam as it is. Don't make it any worse."

"You've got a nerve!"

"Of course I've got a nerve," Roger said impatiently. "All coppers have to have. Why don't you take the one chance you've got?"

Barring didn't speak, but he looked puzzled. His eyes were a muddy brown, and he breathed through very thick lips. Together with his broad nostrils they seemed to indicate a touch of aboriginal blood. Suddenly, it flashed on Roger that this man was not unlike Lancelot Smith.

Roger took the cigarette from his mouth.

"It's probably your last chance," he said. "Please yourself." He half turned.

"Don't move!" Barring ordered.

Roger turned back.

"Get this into your thick head. I'm not going to be frightened by you and I'll leave when I want to. If you use the knife you've got in your pocket you'll sign your own death warrant." He half expected a harsh: *"And yours,"* but it didn't come. "Make up your mind. You can save your neck—if you act soon enough."

"I'll look after my own neck," Barring said, but he was even more puzzled. "Why don't you tell me what's on your mind, West?"

"Make a full statement, name the people you're working for, and give us evidence against them. It couldn't fail to make things easy for you."

"You think you know a lot!"

Roger said: "No one's going to hang me."

Barring began to scowl.

Roger shrugged.

"No one hanged your brother Paul, but he's dead."

Barring's eyes blazed.

"You bloody cops made him do that!"

"No, we didn't," Roger said flatly. "As far as we know, he killed himself. Didn't he know what was in that capsule he swallowed?"

"He knew," Barring asserted as if he was quite sure. "He knew and so did I. You don't know half as much as you think you do, copper. Let me tell *you* something. The Blue Flag Line finished my family. They killed my mother and damned near killed my Dad. They're a murdering lot of thieving swine, and before I've finished with them they won't have a ship left."

"Twenty-seven is a lot of ships to sink," Roger said.

"Twenty-seven, fifty-seven, a hundred and seven—what difference does it make? I tell you there won't be a ship left of the Blue Flag Line." Barring began to draw his hand out of his pocket. "And it won't make any difference to me whether I kill you or not. If it wasn't for you Paul would be alive, and if it wasn't for you I wouldn't be on the run. So I'm going to send you to Paul. Understand? No one gets away with killing a Barring. When the Blue Flag swine swindled the Barring Line they started something they couldn't finish. As long as there's a single Barring left the Blue Flag will——"

Roger half turned again, his right hand at his pocket. Out of the corner of his eye he saw Barring flash the knife, and he dropped flat on to the hard ground. Would Barring throw or stab? Barring was leaping forward, surprised by Roger's move. Roger could see only his legs and feet, and could not tell whether the knife was being plunged downwards. He rolled over, kicking out at Barring's legs. He caught an ankle and heard the man gasp. He pulled the cosh out of his pocket, glimpsed Barring staggering away, with the knife still in his hand.

A man roared: *"What's going on?"*

Roger rolled over again, and sprang to his feet, cosh out. A big man in blue-grey uniform was running along the alley towards them, gun in hand. Barring flung the knife at him, and as he dodged, turned and raced away.

"Get him!" Roger gasped. "That's Marcus Barring. Get him!"

The policeman hesitated, as if too startled to understand. He lost precious seconds, and Barring disappeared.

"I'm West," Roger said, still gasping. "Go get him."

The policeman began to run. Roger backed against a post, drawing in deep, shuddering breaths. He would never know whether the policeman had baulked him of a capture or saved his life. At least he had talked to Marcus Barring, there was a lot he knew now and more he could guess.

Footsteps came clattering. Suddenly the sharp bark of a revolver shot sounded, loud and clear. So there was a chance that Barring would be caught. Roger heard shouts and more footsteps, and thought he heard a splash. If Barring dived into the harbour surely he wouldn't have a chance to get away.

Another policeman came hurrying. Roger straightened up, saw recognition dawn, and knew he would have no problem.

"Are you Superintendent *West*?"

"Yes. Show me what's going on, will you?"

"Trouble down by the Blue Flag Wharf," the policeman said. "This way, sir." They hurried, the policeman always a few paces ahead, until they reached a point from which they could see a large expanse of the harbour, dozens of ships alongside, hundreds of small craft.

Ten minutes later, he learned that Barring had got away.

"You know what I'd call you if I let myself go, don't you?" Luke Shaw, looking as near-angry as he was ever likely to be, was in his big, airy office. Roger sat opposite him. "I'm not sure I shouldn't let myself go, either."

"Save your breath until the conference," Roger said.

"Never mind the conference. If anything happens to you while you're in Australia, we'd never live it down."

"I'll try to leave a parting message absolving you," Roger said. "Promote that policeman who heard me talking to Barring. He saved your reputation as well as my life."

"Why the hell didn't you give me a call?"

"I thought you might have Barring followed."

"I'd have sent a dozen men——" Shaw broke off, and his voice quietened. "There must have been some reason in that bird-brain of yours. What was it?"

"I wanted to give Barring a chance to turn Queen's Evidence."

"Against his *brother*?"

Roger said quietly: "No, his employers. He may have a personal stake in this, but he's being paid, and so was his brother."

"What *is* going on in your mind?" Shaw demanded.

"The same as in yours, or you wouldn't want all twenty-seven Blue Flag ships warned."

Shaw put his head on one side, and began to smile.

"I ought to have known better than to try to fool you, didn't I? Of course it can't be the Barring brothers after the B.F.'s blood. One ship, even two ships—but it's too big for a family like the Barrings."

Roger nodded.

"Any ideas about who is behind it?" Shaw asked.

"Nothing worth calling an idea, except that this is costing a fortune. So it's a big money interest. And there's a measure of desperation in it—kill at all costs, whatever the risk. Family vengeance doesn't operate that way. A few murders among top Blue Flag Line men, stabs in the dark, that kind of thing, yes. But something happened to trigger off the murders of the *Kookaburra* passengers, something sudden, unexpected, urgent. That doesn't fit in with a family feud."

Shaw raised both hands.

"I surrender," he said. "Too right it doesn't. I told you this was too complicated to pass on over the telephone and in reports. But don't make any mistake, Handsome. The Barrings hate the Blue Flag Line. They'll take any risks to get back at it. They may be in someone's pay but they're more than hired killers, they're doing this because they want to. When Marcus Barring says they'll gun for Blue Flag Line ships while there's one of them left, he means it."

"Yes, I suppose so."

"Suppose? It's a dead cert!"

"I had a feeling that when I offered him a chance to turn Queen's Evidence he thought about it," Roger declared. "If we can find a way of offering him the chance again he might take it. Luke, what do you think is behind it?"

"Someone wants to break the Blue Flag Line," Shaw said. "If we rule out the revenge motive, what have we got?"

"Tell me."

"A take-over," Shaw said flatly. "Don't raise your voice, I know what you're going to say! Take-over boys will do any dirty trick to bring down share values before moving in, provided it's legal. They don't go in for wholesale murder."

"Go on," said Roger.

"There've been some queer rumours about some Australian-owned shipping lines," Shaw told him. "Rumours that Red China would like to buy control. Chinese ships can't trade freely, there are a lot of ports they can't go into, and a lot of cargo they can't carry. There isn't much ship-building going on in Chinese yards—it's mostly small stuff. The rumours say that the Chinese would like financial control of some shipping which doesn't carry its flag. They've gone into a lot of mining business in Ceylon and in the Far East, bought their way into a lot of unexpected places, too. We aren't certain, but we think one or two small Australian lines with associations with Hong Kong are Red-controlled. The Blue Flag Line is financed by about sixty per cent Australian—the Flags only—and forty per cent Hong Kong Chinese financiers. There is a lot of Communist infiltration into Hong Kong business and financial life. Fred Hodges gave me some dope on that. I told you he's busy trying to find out more about the Blue Flag Line office in Hong Kong, and he'll dig up plenty. Follow me, Handsome?"

Roger said slowly: "I do indeed."

"You don't sound very convinced."

"Give me time," Roger said. "Red China being so ruthless in getting what she wants, she would be prepared to kill a lot of people to get control. Is that the argument?"

"Are you denying it?"

"Not that it's possible," Roger agreed quickly. "I need a lot of convincing that they'd do it while there's any chance of it being traced back to them."

"They don't think there is," Shaw argued. "If the Barrings have been caught by the Communist bug, that would explain a lot. Why Paul Barring and Lancelot Smith killed themselves rather than be caught, for instance. They didn't trust themselves not to talk, and the Cause was greater than themselves." He paused, but Roger did not speak. Shaw continued: "What do you think, Handsome?"

"Convinced of all this?" Roger demanded.

Shaw grinned.

"No, but it looks the likeliest theory to me. See any rational argument against it as a theory?"

"No."

"We're going to get along," Shaw said, in his half-mocking, half-jocular way. "See why I want every ship warned? Practically all of them—correction—*all* of the ships have Chinese crews, most of them are a hundred per cent Chinese below officer rank. If there's going to be another loss like the *Koala,* it might be any one of the ships. The most obvious thing would be for a member of the crew to blow the vessel up."

"And himself?" Roger objected.

"You don't have much to do with Johnny Chinaman," Shaw declared. "A lot of them are absolute fatalists. They like to think their families are all looked after, but death doesn't worry them. They live too close to it all their lives. Add political fanaticism, and there's your answer."

Roger said: "It certainly could be. You've sold me on one thing, anyhow."

"What's that?"

"Any one of the Blue Flag Line ships could be in danger, anywhere in the world."

Shaw's eyes lit up.

"You'll support me when I ask for all ships to be warned."

"Yes."

"I knew it was right to have you down-under." Shaw

clapped his hands together with a loud bang. "Good on you, Handsome!" After a moment he went on: "Wouldn't like to have a word with the Commissioner now, would you?"

"Let's see if the Blue Flag directors will co-operate first," Roger said.

"Have it your own way," conceded Shaw. He opened a file on his desk. "Now lemme see—ah, here it is. The *Kookaburra* took on the Great Barrier Reef pilot at Thursday Island at six o'clock this morning. They'll be four days coming down to Sydney. All's well on board—the pilot was briefed by the Queensland chaps to do a bit of checking. All the passengers are fit, including the Parrishes."

Roger conceded: "That's something."

"There's a cable in from your chap Kebble, too."

Roger sat up.

"Samuel Hackett has given notice of marriage to a woman named Thérèse Donet in Tours, France."

"Well I'm damned!"

"Doesn't leave him in the clear," Shaw said almost smugly. "But it gave me an idea, Handsome."

"About what?"

"The murders in London and Hong Kong."

"Go on."

"All the passengers known to be coming back to Australia were killed—except the Parrishes. Could that be part of the motive—to kill 'em so as to make sure they couldn't get back here?"

Roger said softly: "It certainly could. I'd missed it."

"It puts the Parrishes on the spot," Shaw said.

"It also puts Doreen Morrison on the spot," Roger said. "It ought to put Limm on it, too." He leaned forward intently. "Anything known about Limm yet?"

"He seems to be what he says he is," answered Shaw, opening a letter. "A sheep farmer from Cowra. Born there, inherited the farm, never been out of Australia before." He pushed a sheet of paper across the desk. "That's a description sent from Cowra. They haven't located a photograph yet but they hope to get it here before the day's out—they'll fly it here if necessary. Judging from that description there isn't much doubt Limm's really Limm, is there?"

"Just enough though," Roger argued.

"The photo will put it beyond any doubt," Shaw said confidently. "The Morrison girls are certainly what they said. So are the Parrishes, although we can't trace Jack Parrish farther back than five years. He settled in Northern Queensland, saying he'd come from South Australia, but no one knows where —yet. Old Sam Hackett came from Western Australia, up near Broome—lost his wife about ten years ago, and turned up in Perth to live on his own. We haven't been able to trace him farther back—yet," repeated Shaw. "He hasn't any relations, and he told his neighbours that all his friends had died, that was why he went South. We're busy on it, and the Western Australia fellows are always on the ball. Sheldon was what he claimed to be, though—insurance agent, unmarried. He had one sister living, no other close relatives. Nothing in his business life to make us suspicious. He put his few belongings into storage—nothing among them to suggest he wasn't what he said he was. He was in shipping and general insurance— worked for a broker in a good way of business. They carried some of the *Koala* loss—but so did dozens of others."

Roger said: "So it's narrowing down."

"So is our time for that conference," Shaw said. "Let's go and have a steak, and then get moving."

17

CONFERENCE WITH V.I.P.S

"BEN," Doreen Morrison said in the husky voice which reflected the nervous tension under which she lived these days, "when is it going to end?"

"It won't be long." Limm tried to reassure her.

"That's what you keep on saying."

"It *can't* be much longer."

She turned away from him and looked over Hyde Park. The private hotel was near Liverpool and Oxford Streets, a clean, pleasant place in a good central position. They had adjoining but not communicating rooms. Along the passage, at the landing, a policeman was on duty all the time. Outside, back and front, there were other policemen. The sun shone on the tops of the trees, and on the grass, but not into this room, which faced east.

It was early afternoon.

"If only we knew why it was happening." A querulous note sounded in Doreen's voice, and there was tightness at her lips; her eyes seemed to hold resentment as well as fear.

"Dorry, my sweet, you must know——"

"Don't keep saying I know!" cried Doreen.

"The secret must be hidden in your mind," insisted Limm doggedly. "They wouldn't try to kill you for no reason at all. Paul Barring was positive someone had told you incriminating things about him—if only you could remember."

"*There isn't anything!*" Doreen raised her voice, and there was a wild look in her eyes. "There just can't be."

"If only we could hit on it——"

"You can't hit on something which doesn't exist!"

"If you would keep on talking about yourself, where you've been, whom you've talked to, you'd suddenly remember some significant thing," went on Limm doggedly. "It's the only way."

"You keep on saying that and I keep on trying!" Tears seemed to shimmer in her eyes. "You keep on making me think of what happened when I was with Denise on the ship, and I want to forget. Can't you understand? I don't want to remember the *Kookaburra,* or anything that happened on it. I just want to forget."

"Yes, I know," Limm said, gently but quite firmly. "You don't want to remember, so you don't remember. But if you could recall it just once and get it out of your system you could forget it for the rest of your life." When she didn't speak, just stared at him with her eyes brimming over, he went on: "You'd feel much better for it, Dorry. While you lock it up in your mind it festers like a sore."

She screwed up her eyes.

"You're only saying this because that man West asked me to remember."

"I'm not," Limm told her positively. "I have strong personal reasons for wanting to know. Dorry, listen. Something you and Denise saw or heard on board that ship almost certainly explains the attacks. Sheldon must have heard it, too, and Neil Sanderson—the First Engineer. You remember Neil. It was probably said when you were all together, having drinks, or having a swim some time. If you could remember it would be like exorcizing a devil."

"All right," Doreen said huskily. "I'll try. I absolutely hate it, because I keep having to think about Denise, and it hurts so much. Can't you understand?"

"You'll never know how much I understand," Limm said. He put his arms round her, held her tightly, and put his lips close to her ear. "Or how much I long to help."

"Good afternoon, gentlemen," said Luke Shaw. "Superintendent West of Scotland Yard made it all right. Mr. West, this is Mr. Raymond Flag, the Chairman of the board."

Raymond Flag was tall, youthful looking, in spite of silvery hair, quite handsome, with a boardroom manner, and a Saville Row look about his clothes. His handshake was firm, his palm cool.

"I am grateful for your readiness to help, Superintendent."

"I'm here to try," Roger said.

"My brother, Gregory, is the Managing Director of the Company," Raymond Flag said.

Gregory was shorter, thickset, dark-haired, forty-ish; a piece of human granite. His handclasp was like the grip of a vice. His fingers had corns and callouses, his face had the weatherbeaten look of the week-end sailor.

"How are you?"

"How're you?" murmured Roger.

"And our cousin, Mortimer Flag, the Company's secretary," Raymond said. "You see, the Blue Flag Line is kept in the family." Mortimer was the youngest, yet running to fat; a good-time boy, Roger thought, fair-haired and pale-faced, but with intelligent eyes despite a weak mouth.

"Do you have absolute control?" asked Roger.

"We have sixty per cent. The rest is shared between our shareholders in Hong Kong and London," answered Raymond. "Come and sit down, Superintendent."

They were in a narrow room, obviously a boardroom. A long window almost filled one wall, with magnificent views over the harbour, perfect today with fleecy clouds in a rich blue, sunlit sky. Eight chairs were gathered about an oval table, and a quick glance told Roger that each chair was different. He made no comment. They all sat down, the Flags obviously in their accustomed places with Raymond in the middle and a Flag on either side of him. Roger and Shaw sat opposite them. In the middle of the figured walnut table was an inlaid map of Australia.

"Is the Commissioner coming?" asked Raymond.

"He couldn't make it," Shaw said.

"A pity. Well, Superintendent"—Raymond looked at Shaw,

not Roger—"I am sure you are as anxious as I to get to business."

"My word, yes." Shaw was almost too emphatic. "Right down."

"Have you any progress to report?"

"Some." Shaw was laconic as he gave details of the attack on Doreen at Hong Kong, and the attack on Roger that morning. All three directors switched their gaze towards Roger. "So we know they're still frightened of the girl, and don't particularly want the Yard to interfere." Shaw looked bland. "I can understand that, can't you?"

"I don't yet understand why Mr. West is here." Mortimer sounded peevish. "Until you arrived these crimes all took place outside this country, didn't they?"

"I'm puzzled, too." Gregory spoke with a bluntness which suited his solid figure. "These were murders committed in England."

"They were indeed." Raymond spread his hands over the desk and the bright polish reflected a gold ring on the little finger of the left hand. "Is there any reason why these crimes should not have had their origin in England? Our resident manager, Lancelot Smith, appears to have felt some responsibility and conceivably connived at the crimes. We have no information about that but consider it most unlikely."

Shaw frowned. Roger sat silent.

"Marcus Barring is wanted for murder and attempted murder, and he came right here to Sydney," Shaw said carefully.

"Couldn't the New South Wales Police have handled that on their own?" inquired Mortimer. Fat and good-time boy he might be, but he was also waspish. "Scotland Yard's responsibility is surely in England, where the crimes were committed. Even the alleged crime at Hong Kong is on a Crown Colony, not in Australia."

Shaw glanced at Roger, who still didn't speak. The attack—and it was an attack—seemed to embarrass Shaw, and he moistened his lips. His voice was gruff.

"We came here to discuss the best thing to do to protect your ships," he said. "Not to try to shelve responsibility."

"*We're* not shelving any responsibility." Mortimer Flag eased his spotless white collar from his pink neck.

"The truth is, Superintendent," Raymond interpolated, speaking mildly and looking so straight at Shaw that it seemed as if he was pretending that Roger wasn't there, "we have spent most of the morning discussing this affair. It appears that one officer of our ships—a man to whom we once had some obligation—was dismissed for bad conduct. His brother, who was a member of the crew, left in protest. Such things have happened before, and doubtless will again. Apparently these men had some reason for hostility to some of the ship's passengers while in England—not on officers or crew, but on passengers. We have come to the conclusion that this is not necessarily connected with the Blue Flag Line, unless you can prove that it is."

He still avoided Roger's eyes.

"I say it is," Shaw asserted roughly. "I say that what happened to the *Koala* could happen to the *Kookaburra*."

"And I say that is nonsense." Raymond Flag's voice was icy.

"It's guff, that's what—plain guff." Gregory shifted his position.

"As the legal authority on the board I have no hesitation in saying that this is guesswork, with no basis in fact," Mortimer stated. "Coming from anyone else it would most certainly be dangerously near slander and defamation."

Shaw's look at Roger seemed to hold appeal, saying it was past time Roger interrupted. Roger sat silent, glancing from man to man, each of whom studiously avoided looking at him, quite sure what he should do.

Shaw took the bull by the horns.

"So you won't co-operate. Is that it?"

"Give us one single reason—valid reason—why we should co-operate and we will do everything we can to help,"

Raymond said smoothly. "Until we have it there is nothing we can do."

"Nothing you *will* do, you mean?" Shaw was nearly out of temper.

Gregory pushed his chair back and stood up.

"Don't be so damned rude. There's nothing we can do because we think you're trying to use us to pull Scotland Yard's coals out of the fire. My God! If the rumour spread around that you thought one of our ships——"

"*All* of your ships, gentlemen." Roger spoke for the first time, so unexpectedly that he startled the others.

"You're out of your mind!" Gregory almost shouted. "If this rumour gets around, what do you think will happen to our stocks? They'll go down with a bang. What do you think will happen to our customers? They'll find other ships. It's difficult enough to get business as things are—with this, it would be ten times worse."

"As it was with the Barring Line before you made them bankrupt," Roger put in.

"It's happened to a dozen shipping companies. It isn't going to happen to this one."

"I wonder." Roger smiled at Shaw and stood up. "We'd better go, Luke."

"Aren't you going to say *any*thing?" Shaw was angry for a different reason now.

"Perhaps Mr. West has nothing to say," Raymond Flag put in sarcastically.

"Not to you, gentlemen," Roger said. "As the Blue Flag Line won't co-operate, we'll obviously have to find someone who will. Those ships have to be warned. There are about four thousand human beings on them, and even if you're not interested in capital loss, other people will be very interested in the loss of human lives."

"There's no one else you can go to," Mortimer said; he was pulling at his collar.

Roger grinned at Shaw.

"Apparently Mr. Flag hasn't heard of the power of the Press. But we really ought to get along. It's getting late." He put a hand on Luke's arm and they turned away. For a moment there was utter silence, and even Luke seemed baffled. Then Roger saw his face split into a grin, and he snorted and smothered a laugh. He opened the door as Raymond Flag called out:

"Are you threatening us?"

Roger swung round on his heel. He felt completely on top of the situation but as he raised his voice his lips twisted, as if he could hardly control his anger.

"No I am not threatening you. I am telling you that in my considered opinion there is lethal danger to one or more ships of your line, and there is no way of finding out which one without your co-operation. So I am going to cable my office in London, and release the story of the danger to the ships. I shall ask all public authorities to co-operate in warning the ships' masters. The London papers will pick the story up within a few hours, all Australian papers will have it in the morning. If that's the kind of publicity you want, that's what you'll get. Your ships must be warned one way or the other."

He turned back to the door.

"Good on you," Luke Shaw whispered.

"You have not yet convinced us that a warning is necessary," Raymond Flag insisted, but there was a placatory note in his voice. "Come and discuss this reasonably."

"Oh, no," Roger said. "Superintendent Shaw used plenty of reason, and you flatly refused to listen. Either we warn the ships through your normal channels by sending coded instructions to the masters for a complete search of each ship for concealed explosives, or we do it through the Press in plain English. Which is it to be?"

The three Flags, Gregory standing, the others sitting, looked at one another with silent admissions of defeat. Raymond made a good effort at least to restore some dignity to the directors' position.

"If the police are so convinced that this is necessary, we will of course co-operate. How soon can you have the message ready for coding?"

Luke Shaw, poker-faced, his jubilation showing only in his eyes, dipped his hand into his pocket, and pulled out a folded sheet of paper.

"Here it is," he said.

Every master of a Blue Flag Line ship received the message by radio that day. Ships in the Indian Ocean, the Pacific, the Atlantic, ships in ports as far apart as London, New Orleans, Hong Kong, Saigon, Buenos Aires, Colombo, Fremantle, and Sydney, all had the message. It read:

> Reason to believe attempt to sink your ship might be made by member of passengers or crew. Carry out comprehensive search for explosive immediately and radio result to Police Headquarters Sydney and a copy to Ocean House.

"Every ship will report all clear," Mortimer Flag said as Roger and Shaw checked over the list of ships and places. "Perhaps you'll then admit that it's a waste of time."

"Let's wait for the result, shall we?" Shaw said bluffly. "Now what we want to know is whether any of you can give us an idea what it's all about."

"We do not think the ships are in danger," Raymond said coldly. "So we certainly can't help you there."

"You don't think the Barring family is gunning for you, do you?"

"We do not," said Raymond. "That is an old affair. We paid the old man a sum in compensation, purely *ex gratia,* and gave those of his sons who wanted a position the security they needed. There is no reason at all to believe that they are carrying out any vendetta."

"Lancelot Smith killed himself," Roger reminded him. "You've seen a note of the statement he made before he died."

"Lancelot Smith suffered from delusions," Raymond declared, still coldly. "We had no reason to think that they

affected his general efficiency. It was Smith who supervised
our take over of the Barring Line. He always felt some degree
of responsibility. Paul and Marcus Barring made some threats
against him, and he was nervous from then on. That is why we
sent him to the London office."

"He stated quite positively that what happened to the *Koala*
could happen to any ship in the line," Roger pointed out.

"He believed the Barrings sank the *Koala*. No one else did.
He roused the suspicions, and as a result there was a delay in
the findings of the Court of Inquiry, but the findings, when
promulgated, were quite clear; there was no evidence as to the
cause. The two Barring brothers ran a launch service at the
Great Barrier Reef, and their launches crossed the *Koala*'s
course. Certainly there was no evidence against the Barrings;
had there been, presumably the police would have acted."

"We'd have acted," Shaw growled.

Five minutes afterwards the two detectives left the office;
no one shook hands, the atmosphere was cold, almost hostile.
They were in a police car outside the office when Shaw spoke
thoughtfully, his jubilation gone.

"They seemed pretty sure of themselves, Handsome. We
couldn't have fooled ourselves, could we?" When Roger didn't
answer, Shaw went on: "If we get an all clear from every
ship, it will look as if they know what they're at. If I'd stuck
my neck out like you did yours, they would be after my
blood."

"They can't get at mine so easily," Roger said mildly.

They settled down, and the chauffeur leaned over and
handed a large envelope to Shaw.

"That was delivered half an hour ago, sir. The messenger
said it was urgent."

Shaw ripped the envelope open, found a photograph, and
pulled it out. It was the right way up, and both men stared at
an unfamiliar face but one which was vaguely like Limm's.

A typewritten note on the back said: *Benjamin Limm, of
Cowra, N.S.W. Now prospecting in North Western Australia.*

"You see that?" breathed Shaw. "Our man isn't Limm."

"Let's get to his hotel, fast," said Roger.

18

ARREST

THE policeman at the front of the little hotel looked drowsy in the afternoon sun, but he straightened up and was alert enough when Shaw and Roger got out of the car and hurried towards him.

"They're both inside," he volunteered.

"Got eyes at the back, too?" demanded Shaw.

"I'd have been told if they'd left, wouldn't I?"

"I hope so," Shaw said forbiddingly.

He led the way in. There was no one in the small office, but a notice said: *'Ring for Service'*. They went upstairs. A policeman at the second landing said:

"All okay, sir."

"Heard anything from them?"

"He's in her room again—spends most of his time there." The man grinned. "Golden opportunity, I'd say."

"No one asked you," Shaw said short-temperedly.

Roger felt the tightening of tension which had been with him so often since the finding of Denise Morrison's body. On the way, misgiving had crowded his mind, too. He would not suffer personally if the Blue Flag Line ships reported all clear, but it would create other problems, and the Flags certainly wouldn't co-operate. He even began to ask himself whether it was possible that Lancelot Smith had suffered from delusions, and whether these killings were divorced from the ships entirely.

They reached the girl's door, which was marked 9.

Shaw banged on it.

There was no immediate response, but a curious kind of noise, almost like a gasp. Then springs, as of a bed, creaked and twanged. Shaw knocked again.

"Who is it?" the man posing as Benjamin Limm called. He sounded out of breath, and now there were other sounds; as of scuffling.

"Superintendent Shaw. I want to talk to you."

"Come back in five minutes," Limm called.

"Open this door in two minutes flat or I'll break it down."

The girl's voice sounded: "*What can they want?*"

Limm didn't answer. Roger heard a soft footfall on the far side of the door and instinctively braced himself. So did Shaw. The door opened inwards, so it couldn't be banged in their faces but Limm might have read the danger signals, and be preparing to rush them.

He stood in the doorway, face dusky red with anger. He had on his trousers, socks, and shirt.

"What the hell do you want?"

"To know who you are," Shaw said curtly. "Cut out the indignation. If you and the girl decide to have a tumble it's no business of ours. What matters is keeping her alive. What's your name?"

"Benjamin Limm?" asked Roger. "Or is it Solomon Barring?"

"Solomon *Barring*!" gasped Doreen.

All the anger drained out of the man's face. Roger realized that he had not anticipated the discovery even after the peremptory call. His colour faded, the aggressiveness in his powerful body died away into consternation.

"Oh no," Doreen whispered. "No."

"You won't alter facts——" Shaw began, but Roger gripped his arm, and he stopped immediately. The two men were on the same wave-length in most things, as Roger had learned when Shaw had visited London.

Benjamin Limm, *alias* Solomon Barring, turned away from them and looked at Doreen. There was something almost pathetic in his attitude. He held his arms out towards her, but not at full length, it was as if he expected a rebuff.

"Dorry, it's not what you think," he said hoarsely. "It is not anything like that."

"You're their brother. And they killed Denise. And I——" Doreen broke off, and looked as if she would burst into tears. Then suddenly fury exploded inside her, she was touched with surpassing beauty as she flung herself at the man. "You devil!" she cried in a shrill, penetrating voice. "You devil."

She struck Solomon Barring in the face, and struck and struck again. He stood without giving ground. She struck again and again until red weals showed, and redder scratches, too, but her lover did not yield at all. The girl raised her hands to strike still more but suddenly dropped them. She turned away from the rumpled bed and stood staring at the wall.

"Dorry," Solomon Barring said, "please listen."

"I don't want to hear."

"Dorry——"

"Go away! I hope I never see you again."

Solomon Barring closed his eyes. He seemed oblivious of the two detectives, of everything except this girl. His lips opened but no words came and he closed them again. Slowly, painfully, he turned away and approached Roger and Shaw. It was a movement of submission, of absolute defeat. He did not speak but gave a little jerky nod.

"I want your explanation," Roger said.

"Not—not here."

"Yes, here."

The man began to show fight.

"No. Let's get out."

"You can't have it all your own way," Shaw said. "We're in a hurry. You're Solomon Barring."

"Yes, I am."

"Why pretend you were someone else?"

"Because—because I didn't want to sail on a Blue Flag ship under my own name."

"Why take Limm's?" Roger demanded.

"For God's sake let's talk about this in the car—anywhere but not here."

"Just talk," Shaw ordered harshly.

Solomon Barring looked as if he would throw himself at them, would do anything to get away, but they blocked his path, two tall and powerful men. He glanced round at the girl, but all she did was to cross to the bed and sit down, her back to the men.

"I believed my brothers were planning some crime against the *Kookaburra*," Solomon said at last. His voice was very hoarse. "Something Paul said one night when he'd had too much to drink made me suspicious. Neither of them would tell me anything." He paused as if he were physically weary, and standing was an ordeal. "At the time of the take-over I hated the Blue Flag Line as much as they did, but I couldn't keep on hating. They could. That's why I moved out to the country, away from Sydney. We didn't meet very often, but whenever we did the subject always came up, and they seemed to get worse instead of better."

"What was your father's attitude?" asked Roger.

"Dad? He just gave up," Solomon said. "The Blue Flag Line gave him a kind of golden handshake, enough to keep him in comfort. Losing the ships hurt him in a lot of ways, but it didn't turn him bad. The worst thing it did was to kill my mother—the worry of it was too much for her. At one time it looked as if the whole family would be without a penny, and Mum and Dad had inherited the Line from their families, it was everything to them. Dad couldn't get a grip on himself for a long time. He went up to the North Coast of Western Australia, did a bit of fishing and played around with the mother-of-pearl business, but it was years before he was anything like himself again. It hurt me to see him. It made my brothers mad. That's the truth—it drove them *mad*. All they could ever think of was revenge."

Solomon stopped, moistened his lips, and shifted his feet.

Doreen was still sitting on the bed, but twisted round, staring at Solomon. Roger stretched out for an upright chair, and pushed it near Solomon.

"I'm all right," Solomon said roughly. He squared his shoulders and stood to his full height. "I heard from a friend in Sydney that they'd got these jobs on the *Kookaburra,* and I didn't like the sound of it. I always had a sneaking fear that they'd had something to do with the loss of the *Koala.* They were running a launch service to Heyman Island at the time, and were less than fifty miles from the spot where she foundered. They wouldn't talk about their reasons for sailing with the *Kookaburra,* so I booked a passage. I borrowed Ben Limm's passport—just stuck my photograph in place of his. Ben is prospecting for uranium up near Cape York, and didn't need it. The issue stamping was about right, and no one ever noticed it. I didn't want Paul and Marcus to know in advance. They didn't know I was on board until we'd been at sea the better part of a day."

"What did they do?" Roger asked.

"They told me I was wrong to be suspicious, and they were going to work for Blue Flag in future. They said they'd got over their thirst for revenge."

"Did you believe them?"

"No."

"Did you see any evidence of what they were planning?"

"I don't really know," Solomon said, heavily. He looked round at Doreen, as if the way she was now staring at him had made him sensitive. The expression in his eyes grew brighter and his voice became stronger. "At the end of the voyage Paul was seen entering passengers' cabins, and he had a passenger's wallet in his own berth. The passenger wouldn't make a charge, and Paul had to leave the ship at Southampton. Marcus went with him. They'd talked big to Denise and Doreen on the ship, and I tried to discourage the girls, but they wouldn't listen. When I saw Denise's photograph in the newspaper, I just had to know what had happened to Doreen, so I came and saw you. I couldn't tell all the truth but I told as much of it as I could. I didn't believe Paul was a murderer. I can hardly believe it even now."

Doreen stood up from the bed, very slowly.

"You said you didn't really know if you saw any evidence against your brothers," Roger said.

"I thought possibly they'd decided to steal from the passengers, making things as unpleasant for the line as possible," Solomon said. "Now it's obvious there was more to it than that, and entering cabins and stealing that wallet may have had something to do with it. As for why they killed Denise and tried to kill Doreen, and why they killed Sheldon—I simply don't know. In London——" He hesitated again, and glanced round; Doreen was within arm's reach. He stretched out, and she took his hand. "In London I simply didn't know what to do. I told you who—who Denise was. I hoped—I prayed—that my brothers had nothing to do with her murder, but now I know they had. The one thing I could do was try to help Doreen. I felt sure she must know why it had happened even if she didn't realize it. You"—he looked at Roger—"you asked me to try to make her talk, but I didn't need any persuasion. She can't remember anything that might help, that's the hell of it. Can you, Dorry?"

"If only I could," she said. Her voice was stronger and her manner had a new self-assurance. "I've racked my brains but I can't think of a thing anyone told me about those two. Ben"— she did not seem to realize that she used his false name—"why didn't you tell me?"

"Would you really have believed me?" Solomon asked. "Would it really have been better to know who I was? I wanted to make you remember, because it seemed the only way I could save you from harm."

His manner, his eyes, his voice, all added: "Because I love you so much."

"Just one more question," Roger said. "Do you know why your brothers didn't attack you?"

After a long silence, Solomon Barring answered: "They wouldn't kill me. That's the last thing they'd do. The family mattered so much to them. They wouldn't kill me in any circumstances. They'd take it for granted I wouldn't harm them, either." He squared his shoulders. "You'll make sure Doreen is safe while I'm away, won't you?"

"Where are you planning to go?" asked Luke Shaw.

"Aren't you going to take me with you?"

"We're going to watch you closely, and we want you to stay here until we've cleared up some points," Luke said. "So far we may have suspicion but we haven't any case against you."

"The best thing you can do is to try to jog Doreen's memory," Roger said emphatically. "Even a word or two might be enough to help us. One question, now."

"Yes?"

"Do you know where we might find your brother Marcus?"

"If I did I'd take you to him," Solomon Barring declared. "I haven't the faintest idea."

It was some time before either Shaw or Roger spoke, when they had left the room. Roger felt strangely affected both by the story and by the reconciliation between the man and Doreen. There was some quality about their obvious love for each other which had a humbling effect on him.

"I think he was telling the truth," said Shaw abruptly, when they were in the hotel hall.

"It would surprise me if he wasn't," Roger admitted. "How soon can you check with the real Limm?"

"Shouldn't take long," Shaw said. "I'll get it started as soon as I'm back in the office. You any ideas?"

"My only idea is to speed up the answers from those ships," Roger said.

"Should be coming in by now." Shaw stepped on to the pavement of Liverpool Street and saw the mass of home-going traffic between them and the park, screwed up his nose and remarked: "Be quicker to walk than take the car."

"Suits me," said Roger. "Do you know what we haven't had time to do?"

"Digest the developments of the conference with the Flags," answered Shaw, with a nod. "We'll have to see what the old sub-conscious has done for us. When you called their bluff they caved in pretty quick."

"Too quick?" wondered Roger.

"Don't be cryptic. Tell you what," went on Shaw, "let's shut up until we're back in the office. We can't talk here."

He was right. The pavements were thicker with people than the roads with cars. There was the constant hum of engines, clatter of footsteps, medley of other noises. Shaw kept just ahead, and Roger had difficulty in keeping pace, so many people got in their path. It was relaxing in a way—physical exertion and stimulation yet a rest for his mind. They seemed to be walking past shops for a long time until they came to the narrow street which led to the police headquarters. This was almost empty, a temporary backwater. They turned into the crowded parking place of the building and went up in a lift which crawled. Shaw drummed his fingers on the back of his hand, betraying his impatience. They got out at the third floor, and walked straight to his office. It was empty. The papers on the desk were tidy, and on top of one file was a pencilled note, much as Kebble would have left it in Roger's office. Almost indifferently Shaw picked it up and read it. The change in his manner was astounding.

"The bloody swine," he rasped. "Marcus Barring rang up, and sent a message to you *and* me." Roger streaked across the room, and read as Shaw went on: "He says the *Kookaburra* will never tie up again. And if I know Barring, he means it."

19

MESSAGES FROM SHIPS AT SEA

As Roger read and Luke Shaw talked, a man appeared at the doorway. Roger noticed him first. He was a stranger, tall and well-dressed, Raymond Flag in build and appearance but in a less unctuous way. He looked very alert as he came in, iron-grey hair brushed straight back from a broad forehead. His eyes were deepset, very brilliant blue.

Luke Shaw snapped almost to attention.

"Good evening, sir."

"Hallo, Luke." The newcomer advanced towards Roger, hands outstretched; a remembered photograph and Luke's manner told Roger this was Hugh Petherell, the Commissioner of Police for New South Wales. "Sorry I couldn't meet you earlier, Superintendent." His handclasp was very firm. "You've talked to Marcus Barring, I understand. Do you think this is a genuine message or a hoax?"

"I think he thinks that what he says is true," answered Roger.

"*Thinks?*"

"'He believes the *Kookaburra* will sink before she ties up again."

"Wouldn't he know for certain?"

"I don't see how we can be sure that he does," reasoned Roger. "I'd take it very seriously indeed."

"My God, so would I," Luke breathed.

The Commissioner was looking at Roger, now unsmiling.

"I'm told you persuaded the Flags to make a decision they had no liking for," he said. "So if there is trouble on board the *Kookaburra,* a search should reveal it. If it doesn't, the Flags will say the whole thing is a hoax aimed at their good name and their goodwill."

"Do they know about this message?"

"No," Petherell said. "I telephoned Raymond Flag to tell him that I had reason to believe there was danger, that is all. How widespread is your search for Marcus Barring, Luke?"

"As wide as I can make it."

"Statewide, do you mean?"

"Nationwide."

"We must find him," Petherell said. "The search must have absolute priority." Obviously he was deeply worried. "What have you new for me?"

He sat on a corner of the desk, expectantly. Shaw reported the interview with the Flags and the development with Solomon Barring. Petherell frowned in concentration throughout that story.

"And you left Solomon Barring at the hotel?"

"Yes."

"Get him here," Petherell demanded. "There's no way of being sure that he's telling the truth." There was an edge of reprimand in his voice. "One of his brothers sacrificed his life, so did Lancelot Smith. Solomon might murder this girl knowing he can't get away with it. Bring him in at once and hold him for questioning."

Luke looked at Roger, in a kind of sardonic appeal.

"What do you think, Handsome?"

"It can't do any harm even if I don't think it will do any good," Roger conceded.

"It will make sure that we don't lose Doreen Morrison by our own neglect," Petherell said decisively. "That's a chance I'm not going to take."

Luke Shaw's hand was already on the telephone.

"I quite understand why you have to do this," Solomon Barring said. "It doesn't alter the fact that I have told you the whole truth."

"Haven't you any idea at all where we might find your brother?" Roger demanded.

"None at all."

"No old haunts or familiar places?"

"None that aren't known to anybody. The Surf Club, the Sydney Yacht Club, the Skin Divers Club—but he couldn't hide out in any of these."

"Any girl friends? Women friends?"

"No steadies. Marcus always took his pleasures where he could find them," Solomon Barring said bitterly. "If I could help you I would. You can't want to see this thing through more than I do."

"Did your brother have many friends?"

"He hasn't been in Sydney much for the past ten years. I doubt if he's seen any of his old friends since we had to sell out. Not that he ever had many friends. He always had to do everything better than anyone else, which didn't exactly make him popular."

"All the same we'd better question as many as we can," Luke said. He was smarting under Petherell's implied rebuke. "Make out a list, will you?"

"If I must," Solomon said. "Superintendent——"

"Yes?"

"Don't let anything happen to Doreen."

"She's under full protection."

"She'd better be."

"Barring, hasn't she recollected anything to give a clue?" Roger asked.

"Nothing—absolutely nothing," Solomon assured him with obvious conviction. "I don't think she will, now. I'm beginning to wonder whether there was anything for her to remember."

"So am I," Roger said softly. "There may be a way to find out. We missed it earlier. Can you call on a good psychiatrist to probe into her mind?" he added to Shaw.

"Can do," Shaw answered at once. "We may have missed it but we haven't had much time. I'll fix it. If Doreen hasn't got anything to remember it would make nonsense of the whole affair." After a moment's hesitation he turned away. "I must get cracking. Don't miss anyone off that list of old-time friends of your brother, Barring."

"They won't do anything to Ben, will they?" Doreen Morrison hadn't yet fully accepted her lover's new identity. "He told you the truth, I'm sure he did."

"I think so too," Roger reassured her. "And if he didn't, he's in no danger from the police. Doreen, do you realize what might be at stake?"

"The *Kookaburra*, and everyone on it."

"Or an even bigger ship," Roger said. "We're going to get a psychiatrist to try to help you. Co-operate in every possible way, won't you? It will not only help the ship, it might help to prove that Ben is telling the truth."

Jack and Jill Parrish stood on the deck of the *Kookaburra*, early next morning, Saturday, arms about each other as if the moon, not the rising sun, was spreading light over them. Near by, three sailors were checking the provisions in a lifeboat.

"Three more days and three more nights," Jack Parrish said. He was looking at his young wife's profile. "Then a week in Sydney and a last shopping spree, before life among the bananas!"

"Don't make me eat too many," Jill said. "Darling, did you notice anything strange yesterday?"

"No. Did you?"

"There seemed such a bustle among the crew—and our cabin hasn't been cleaned so thoroughly since we came aboard."

"Spring cleaning, because the V.I.P.s might come aboard for an inspection," Jack said. "They're even going over the lifeboats again, although they checked them just out of Hong Kong. Just as well they're thorough."

Marcus Barring, unaware of the fact that over the years his hatred of the Blue Flag Line had become an obsession, swam from the little beach near Sydney Heads with the long, deliberate strokes of the swimmer who was absolutely at home in the water. Near by were some rocks, popular with goggle-fishers and underwater swimmers, and used by beginners in skin-diving. Today he wore goggles, with the breathing tube inches above the water, and flippers. If every policeman in Sydney had seen him then they would not have recognized him, he felt absolutely confident of that, confident enough to boast about what he was going to do. He had to boast, had to talk on the telephone at the very least; bottling everything up inside him was impossible. He could still remember how shocked the policeman he had talked to had sounded. He felt absolutely secure.

The Water Police in the launch carrying out their part in the great search for the wanted man, did not give this skin-diver a second thought. After all, there were eight or nine others within sight.

Marcus Barring was making quite sure he knew the effect of the currents and of the swell just inside the Heads.

The first radio telegram from a Blue Flag Line ship reached Police H.Q. at a quarter past three that Saturday morning. It said: *Search completed, nothing found. Master, Nesia.* By the time Roger reached the office, at a quarter to eight, eleven 'all clear' messages were in, but none from the *Kookaburra.* A sergeant brought in two more. *The Reef,* in dock at Hong Kong was clear, so was *The Tasman,* now sailing between Bombay and Colombo.

At half past eight, Luke Shaw arrived.

"Don't look so smug, I've been down to the harbour and had a talk with the Water Branch," he said. "They've searched every small ship, every possible hiding-place along the shore line, and they've found no sign of Barring. The devil can't have disappeared into thin air." As he spoke the sergeant came in again. "Anything from the *Kookaburra* yet?"

"No. *The Adela*'s clear, in Saigon."

"How many does that make?"

"Fourteen."

"Over halfway. Any word from that psychiatrist, Handsome?"

"I saw him at ten o'clock last night," Roger answered. "Nothing doing yet."

"Does *he* think she's got anything tucked away in her mind?"

"He thinks she might have."

"Fat lot of help that is," Shaw gloomed. "Well, he's got the week-end to work in, and so have we. It's a good job we know the *Kookaburra*'s been warned, if we didn't I'd fly up to her myself."

"Where is she?"

"About two hundred miles north of Brisbane," Shaw answered. "She's due to berth on Tuesday, early afternoon. We can't do a thing except work over all we know, check with Hong Kong, and make sure we're all set to act on Monday morning."

"We can cable the Yard to go over everything at Smith's office with a fine-toothed comb," Roger said. "And we can get them to check whether there's any sign of Communist influence at the Blue Flag Line office there. Fred Hodges will have more time to work on Wu Hong, too. Where shall we work from?"

"Better spend the week-end at my place," Luke said. "At least we'll have some comforts between telephone calls."

Fifi Shaw could not have made Roger more welcome; they even found time, on the Sunday afternoon, to drive up to Palm Beach and look in at the surfing at all the beaches on the way. Word came from more and more ships that no explosives had been found after a thorough search.

They were in the office early on the Monday morning, edgy because the only word from the *Kookaburra* was that the search was proceeding. There were piles of papers on Luke

Shaw's desk, almost as many on Roger's. Most were routine reports, details of the ship's searches. Roger made hardly any notes as he read on.

Shaw looked up, a file under his hand. "We've questioned twenty-nine of Barring's old buddies, and none of them have seen him for five years or more." He studied another report. "The real Benjamin Limm confirms Solomon's story about the passport, the police up at Broome have interviewed him. Damned fool." Shaw put those papers aside and picked up another file. Roger saw his body stiffen. "Here's a queer one."

Roger went across to him, heart leaping.

"Good or bad?"

"Remember Percival Sheldon?"

"He was in insurance in Adelaide, and murdered at London Airport," Roger said.

"Good on you." Shaw looked up, frowning, but a hint of excitement showed in his eyes. "He was a friend of Mortimer Flag. How about that?" He squatted on the corner of his desk. "I wonder if those baskets know more than we realize. How would you like a chance to put Mortimer through a nice fine screen, the fat so-and-so."

"Don't you want it?" asked Roger. "Where's that list of members of the Sydney Yacht Club?" As Shaw handed it to him he flipped over the pages to the *Fs*.

"I've got to see the Commissioner at nine-thirty, and I ought to be around until all the reports are in from the ships. Go and see Mortimer, Handsome. If there's any news, I'll call you."

Roger said softly: "I'll gladly go. Mortimer Flag is about Marcus Barring's age, which is thirty-nine. Percival Sheldon was thirty-eight. All three were members of the Yacht Club, as well as in the same age-group. Did they have anything else in common, I wonder."

Mortimer Flag was in his own office, which was large, shiny, almost flashy. A big portrait of Raymond Flag, the silvery hair showing that it had been painted recently, hung on the wall behind the desk. There was a huge slab of plate glass over it. To call him fat would be unjust, but he would soon become fat if he went on as he was doing. His dark hair was slicked down, his pale face had the smoothness of a woman's— almost as if he did not need to shave.

"Yes, I knew Sheldon as a club member," he said to Roger. "Is there any reason why I shouldn't?" That was a poor attempt at sarcasm. "I also knew Marcus Barring."

"Was there any association except in the club?" asked Roger.

"We were known to play cards together."

"You mean you gambled?"

"With modest stakes, yes. I really cannot see the relevance of these questions. All of this is old history. We haven't met for over ten years."

"When you broke up the Barrings' business——"

"Let me make one thing crystal clear," interrupted Mortimer. He acquired a kind of dignity which Roger had not seen in him before. "We did *not* break up the Barring Line. It was an old-fashioned, badly managed company, seriously undercapitalized. In order to meet increasing competition, the Line borrowed too heavily and incurred a number of debts it could not pay. When we acquired it, we paid off all debts, gave old Barring generous compensation, and later even made room for the sons in this company, when they were in need. There is no guilty conscience among the directors of this company, Superintendent."

Roger said mildly: "That's good, sir. It's always easier to work with all the cards on the table. You were friendly with Marcus Barring before the take-over, then. Were you afterwards?"

"No. He took the take-over as a personal affront and behaved like a fool."

"Whose side was Sheldon on?"

"As far as I know he took a completely rational view. He

moved to Adelaide soon afterwards, and continued to do considerable business for the Line. That is no secret. We met perhaps twice a year."

"Did you ever notice any change in his attitude towards you?"

"None at all."

"Why did he travel on the *Kookaburra*?"

"He had a serious operation for lung cancer last year, was advised to take a long sea trip, and was able to go on the Blue Flag Line at a nominal cost." Mortimer Flag's little, feminine mouth was pressed so tightly that the lips seemed to disappear. "Where *is* all this leading to?"

"I want to know what other interests you, Sheldon, and Marcus Barring had in common, what friends you had, whether there was any reason other than the take-over for Barring's deep-rooted enmity."

"We had no other interests—except a love of swimming, surfing, and sailing. We were members of the same surf, swimming, and yachting clubs. If you get lists of the members of the clubs twelve years ago you will find all the information I can give you. Now you must excuse me, Superintendent. I have an important board meeting in twenty minutes' time."

"I won't keep you long," Roger said. "One more question."

"Very well."

"Are you considering any offer for a take-over, Mr. Flag?"

Flag snapped: "No, we are not."

"Hasn't it been on the agenda?"

"No!"

"Then what made you think that the whole purpose of the *Kookaburra* murders might be an attempt to weaken your standing? Your cousin Gregory was most concerned as to what would happen if the stories got around—too concerned, some might think. So were you. A company in good standing can weather a temporary recession, but a company which wants to preserve itself and its assets including goodwill could suffer from rumours very seriously. Why are you so nervous, Mr. Flag?"

Mortimer Flag stood up, very slowly, moistened his lips, held his right lapel tighter, showing how plump and pale his hand was, and spoke with unexpected dignity.

"I am not nervous. Nor are my fellow directors. We are jealous, extremely jealous, of our good name. We do not believe there is anything for us to fear. We believe that if you, the police, did your job properly you would find that these murders are not associated with the Blue Flag Line. If you wish to see me in the future, Superintendent, I must ask you to make a formal appointment. Now I must ask you to——"

His telephone bell rang. He hesitated, then leaned forward, and picked up the instrument.

"I told you I wanted no interruptions. . . . I see. . . . Yes, in those circumstances you were quite right." He held out the telephone. "The call is for you."

"Thanks." Roger took the receiver, and in doing so touched Mortimer Flag's hand; it was warm and moist. He gave that a passing thought as he said: "West speaking."

"Handsome, it looks as if we're coming unstuck," Luke Shaw said in a voice which betrayed real anxiety. "We've had all the radio reports in now, and every ship is clear—including the *Kookaburra*, which is due in on Monday, a day early."

It was now Monday morning, time was running so very short.

20

JUBILATION TO DESPAIR

MORTIMER FLAG, still standing at the desk, stared intently at Roger. Roger had the impression that the director already knew the result of the searches, and was now looking for signs of defeat; was beginning to gloat. Roger swallowed his pride, and said:

"Every ship completely clear. Is that it?"

"That's it. Almost wish one would blow up," Shaw said lugubriously. "Thought I'd better let you know in case the Flags know already. You'll realize it won't be any use trying to ride rough-shod over them. Sorry I got you into this spot, Handsome."

Roger laughed, honestly amused.

"If that's the worst that ever happens to me, I'll be lucky. I'll be seeing you." He replaced the receiver, and smiled at Mortimer Flag. "All your ships report clear," he said.

Mortimer's eyes were glowing.

"That's wonderful!" So he hadn't known. "I told you you were making a mares' nest." He lifted a telephone, but before he spoke the door behind Roger opened and Raymond Flag appeared. Roger, looking over his shoulder, saw the chairman's eyes glowing, and the look of triumph on his face. Just behind him Gregory Flag was grinning with delight.

"All absolutely clear," Raymond crowed.

"God, what a relief!" exclaimed Gregory.

Roger moved so that his back wasn't to any of them. He had expected to find gloating; in fact, he found what seemed to be unfeigned relief, remarkable in men who had appeared so confident that there could not possibly have been trouble on any of the Blue Flag Line ships.

"Surprised, Superintendent?" asked Raymond. "I suppose that's natural. We believed you were wrong, but when you were so insistent you really had us worried. This is a great relief."

"Even if it disappoints Superintendent West," Mortimer put in waspishly.

"If I've given you the impression that I wanted one of your ships to vanish with all hands, I did a bad job," Roger said. "This may remove your main anxiety, but it doesn't remove mine. I want to catch a killer. I need men with money who are behind the killer, and I need to know why the murders were committed, why Lancelot Smith warned me that any of your ships might go down, and——"

"I've told you, Smith was obsessed with delusions," Raymond interrupted.

"Do you think that's why Marcus Barring telephoned Superintendent Shaw and told him that the *Kookaburra* would never tie up in Sydney Harbour again?" asked Roger.

"I don't believe——" Gregory began, but his voice trailed off.

"*What?*" gasped Mortimer.

"When was this?" demanded Raymond Flag.

All their jubilation vanished; in an instant their mood changed completely, alarm if not consternation was in their manner. They had moved so that they were lined up on one side of Mortimer's desk and Roger was on the other, his back to the door.

"It was immediately after I made an issue of the searches," Roger said. None of the others spoke, and into the tense silence he dropped a question he had been wanting to ask ever since he had known these men. "There are rumours that Chinese interests in Pekin would like to acquire the Blue Flag Line, and are attempting to force you to sell just as you forced the Barrings to sell. Have you been under any such pressures?" When none of them answered, he went on: "The kind of sacrifices made by Lancelot Smith and Paul Barring square with fanatical political faith. Have you any reason to believe that Smith was a Communist?"

Gregory Flag said: "My God!"

Mortimer moved across to an easy-chair in the window, and dropped down into it.

Raymond stood at the desk, very pale, very still. It seemed a long time before he spoke, a long time before he could make up his mind what to say. When the words did come they were low-pitched and uttered in a voice empty of emotion.

"Yes," he said.

Roger, touched by the tension, made himself speak harshly.

"Are you sure he was?"

"Yes."

"Did you know he was involved in some conspiracy against the company?"

Raymond answered: "We feared it."

"Why?"

"We know he wanted us to sell a majority of our holdings to Chinese nominees. We refused. When these crimes were perpetrated, we feared that an attempt was being made to force our hands."

"When did this pressure begin?"

"Six months ago."

"After the S.S. *Koala* sank?" asked Roger.

"Yes," Raymond said. "In fact that——"

"Raymond, there's no need for this," Mortimer said. He jumped up from the chair looking pale, but as if he were ready to put up a fight. "There is no need for any further admissions or statements. There have been enough. We've done everything humanly possible to make sure nothing goes wrong. Let matters rest as they are."

"You didn't do much about warning your ships' masters, although you must have feared danger to one or another of them," Roger said harshly.

"We knew perfectly well that if you wanted the warnings sent out you would send them out, it was immaterial whether we liked it or not," Mortimer said coldly. "Your way it was a police inquiry. Had it been sent out by us it would have implied our belief that there was some danger. No such admission was necessary. We are not fools, Mr. West."

"I wonder."

"What the hell do you mean?" Gregory Flag roared.

"You must be fools if you really doubt whether I know that severe pressures made you keep silent, refusing to admit there was any danger. Obviously the pressure first made itself felt six months ago, nearly eighteen months after the loss of the

Koala. They must have been very severe to affect you so badly. I'd say you were blackmailed."

"I won't listen to this nonsense!" cried Mortimer. He jumped up and came forward, podgy hands clenched. "You have no right to slander——"

"Oh, shut up," Roger said angrily. "I can say what I like to the three of you, there's no question of slander. If it ever came to a court of law you'd be three to one against me, so I couldn't bring it to court. The *Koala*'s sinking was an insurance fraud, wasn't it?"

"Don't say a word!" cried Mortimer. "Deny it."

Neither of the others spoke, but Raymond slowly turned way. After a moment, he asked:

"Who else suspects this?"

"Never mind that," Roger rasped. "The *Kookaburra* is under threat. She's been reported all clear and yet she's still under threat. You know it. You expected something to be found aboard, that was why you were so elated when you had the all clear. Was the *Kookaburra* your second insurance swindle? Was she to go down with all passengers and all hands to make some more filthy money for you?" When no one responded he raised his voice and shouted: "Is that the truth? Answer, damn you, answer me!"

"Don't—don't say a word," Mortimer almost choked.

After another long pause, Raymond Flag turned round, faced Roger squarely, and said:

"There is nothing we can do to stop it, West. We don't know what Marcus Barring plans, we have no idea how he meant to carry his plans out. There is nothing at all we can do."

"We didn't know what he planned!" Mortimer said gaspingly. "Greg—make Ray stop. He mustn't say another word. Make him stop."

The Flag brothers now stared at each other, as if in fear.

Roger said savagely: "I don't know what you've got on

your conscience. But if another man dies, if another man is injured, my God you'll pay for it."

"I tell you we don't know where to find Barring!" That was Raymond.

"Was he to blow up the *Kookaburra* for you?"

"Don't say a word!" screeched Mortimer.

"You must know what he planned. How was he going to do it?" Anger, half simulated, half real, made Roger's voice hoarse. Recollection of the positive relief these men had shown when told nothing had been found on any ship made one thing obvious. They had expected a time-bomb or some such device inside the ship before it reached Sydney, but did not necessarily know anything more. If he could frighten them enough they might yet tell him what Marcus Barring planned.

A telephone bell rang, a jarring, unwanted sound from outside. Gregory Flag moved and plucked up the instrument, snatching at any release from tension. Mortimer moved towards his elder cousin, hands stretched out as if in supplication. There could be no doubt of the awful guilt of these three men, but that hardly seemed important; retribution could come later, rescue from that unknown danger was desperately needed first.

"Yes?" Gregory Flag's voice rose high. "Who? ... Yes, hold on." He lowered the receiver and handed it towards Roger. "It's Shaw, for you."

Roger took the telephone, and said as mildly as he could: "Yes, Luke?"

"We've had a break," Shaw said with suppressed excitement. "That psychiatrist made something click in Doreen Morrison's memory. She remembers a quarrel between Perce Sheldon, the Adelaide insurance man and Paul Barring. She doesn't know what it was about, but she remembers some of the words. Your psychiatrist thinks some are probably key words. Ready for 'em?"

"Yes," Roger said.

"Sheldon shouted the words: *'Yes, all of them, damn you, all of them. You'll never get away with it.'*"

Roger had a pencil out and wrote swiftly in a kind of private shorthand.

"Next?"

"Paul Barring responded calmly: *'Nothing you or anyone else can do will stop us. You'd better not try.'*"

"Go on," Roger said tensely. He was aware of the others drawing nearer, as if in an effort to see what he was writing.

"Sheldon replied, wildly: *'You can't scare me. Too many people know. Don't open your bloody mouth, understand?'*"

"Yes," Roger said.

"That's it." Shaw seemed almost reluctant to finish. "Someone else came along—the Captain or first mate, Doreen thinks, and the shouting stopped. Next time Sheldon and Paul Barring met they were drinking together, and seemed on friendly terms. Doreen says she forgot everything about this until the psychiatrist questioned her about conversations she had heard between other people. Then it came back to her. See the significance, don't you? Sheldon's 'all of them' could have meant the people who afterwards died. Paul Barring's 'You'd better not try to stop us,' could be the threat to kill. Sheldon or any of the people he was supposed to have informed could have become a danger to the Barrings."

"But did Sheldon tell the girl anything?" Roger asked.

He looked up as he spoke, into the faces of the three men. Mortimer's face blanched, he opened his lips and gasped; and he seemed to form the name 'Sheldon'.

"She can't remember anything. Of course Sheldon may have been lying," went on Shaw. "He may have told Paul Barring that those other people knew, simply to scare Barring. If he did, and if Barring had to go ahead with whatever he planned—the sinking of the *Kookaburra*, say—he may have killed them all to make sure none of them could stop him."

"So all the murders would be directly concerned with the plot against the *Kookaburra*," Roger said. "Right, Luke, thanks. We need a full transcription of everything Sheldon said, of course."

"What's that?" asked Shaw, puzzled.

"I'll be in touch," Roger said.

He rang off, still watching the three directors closely. They looked sick with fear, but Raymond had a better grip on himself than the others. Mortimer had given up trying to stop him from speaking.

"So Sheldon was in the insurance swindle over the *Koala*, and knew about the plot on the *Kookaburra*," Roger said coldly. "Paul and Marcus Barring decided to kill everyone he said he had told."

"We knew nothing about such a decision," Raymond Flag asserted. "We had reason to suspect that in his obsessive hatred for this company, Marcus Barring would try to blow up a second ship. Insurance was not involved. In spite of the Court of Inquiry findings we suspected sabotage on the *Koala*, as did the police. None could be proved. We had reason to fear further sabotage for the same reason on the *Kookaburra*, but we could do no more than we did—you were in fact ahead of us. We are not criminals. If we knew how to stop this wickedness we would have told you long ago. We believed that some time bomb would be planted on the ship, as you did. If that isn't the case——"

He broke off.

Roger caught his breath, and turned to the telephone, snatched it up and barked: "Get me Superintendent Shaw, of Police Headquarters." He held the receiver to his ear. "If it isn't an inside job it's an outside one. Marcus Barring's an expert goggle-fisher and underwater swimmer. One limpet mine on the hull of the *Kookaburra* would be enough to sink her. What time is she due?"

"She's picking up the pilot outside the Heads about now," Raymond said.

21

LIMPET

"LUKE," Roger said, "one limpet mine on the hull of the *Kookaburra* would sink it."

"And do God knows what damage to the nearest houses," Shaw said tautly. "We've got all the Water Police launches and a dozen naval frogmen almost ready to go. You nagged about Marcus Barring's past so much, I really got down to checking it. He was an expert skin-diver and trained as an amateur frogman. I'm going to pick up a launch at Circular Quay right now. Coming?"

"If you don't wait for me it will be the last time I'll come to Sydney."

"I'll leave a smaller launch, you can catch up," Luke said.

Roger put down the receiver, very slowly. Everything in him screamed 'hurry', but Shaw and the others could handle the crisis in the harbour better than he. His first job was with the Flags. Raymond had regained his poise and was fighting back. Mortimer was looking better, as if he had been drawn safely from the brink of a precipice. Gregory stood, block-like, by the window looking out over the harbour.

"So you think that's how he will do it," Raymond said levelly. "I know the police will do everything humanly possible to save the ship. There is nothing at all we can do."

"No," Roger agreed in a cold, hard voice. "Nothing you can do—except hire the best lawyers in Australia to try to get you cleared of a charge of multiple murder."

"We have committed no crime," Raymond said.

"You haven't enough evidence even to make a charge, and if a rumour of what you've been saying leaks into the newspapers, we'll sue you for a million pounds for defamation—you *or* Scotland Yard."

"You won't need to," Roger said. "You keep busy working on your defence."

He saw Gregory's hands clenching by his side. Gregory looked the strongest but might prove to be the weakest of them all. It would be useless to try to work on him now, for under the protection of his brother and his cousin he would hold out. Expecting him to crack was probably a forlorn hope, anyhow.

Roger turned towards the door. None of the others came back at him, that last thrust had worried them. He went out, his heart like a leaden weight with a sense of utter failure. Failure was always bitter. He hadn't even been the first to jump to the limpet mine possibility. It had been so obvious once he had thought of it, but if no action had been taken before it had sprung to his mind, what chance would there be to save the *Kookaburra*?

What chance was there now?

Roger began to think of that, and preoccupation with his own failures faded. He kept his finger on the bell-push for the lift, but one was a long time coming. He glanced out of a narrow window on the landing, and suddenly realized he could see the Heads. He strode to the window and looked over the sunlit city towards the Bridge and the harbour. There could be no better view, but he wasn't interested in the scene, only in the ship which was through the great cliffs of the entrance and well into the harbour.

Small craft were approaching it.

A girl called: "Going down."

Roger turned and half ran to the lift.

Jack and Jill Parrish and all the other passengers of the *Kookaburra* stood on deck, watching the passing scene: the bays and inlets, the small craft at anchor, the cliffs, and the rocks. The sun was warm but not hot; it was quite, quite beautiful.

They put down the hustle and bustle about them to preparations for berthing, although they knew they had to go under the Bridge for the ship would tie up in the inner harbour.

Then quite unbelievably, the signal to abandon ship broke through the idyllic minutes. Six short, one long blast on the ship's whistle, which did not seem to stop. They saw many of the boats heading towards them, and Parrish recognized a naval launch equipped for deep-sea diving.

"It can't be serious," Jill said, half scared.

"It's serious, all right," Jack said. "Come on."

As in a dream turned nightmare they hurried down to their cabin for lifebelts. Other passengers appeared, puzzled, some frightened looking. A young officer said:

"No need to be alarmed. There's plenty of room for all, and we haven't far to go."

Some Chinese crew were running purposefully.

Someone laughed, on a note of hysteria.

Someone called out in a clear, high-pitched voice:

"What about the *sharks*?"

The alarm signal, the young officer, the word 'sharks', and thought of all her trousseau—practically everything she possessed—being lost, all merged together in Jill Parrish's mind as she hurried along, her husband's fingers tight about her forearm. The sounds so often heard at sea, of the lifeboats being lowered from the davits, became suddenly sinister.

"Hurry!" she gasped. "We've got to hurry!"

She was gasping for breath as panic began to work in her.

"I shall stay with the ship," the Master said into the loudspeaker. "All passengers and members of the crew will abandon ship. All officers may do so when their duties are completed."

The sun was so warm. The harbour so beautiful. The Bridge so unbelievably huge, as if indestructible. Cars were flashing across it, and in the distance he could hear the rumble of a train.

Marcus Barring reached the *Kookaburra* ten minutes before the alarm was given. He was no longer excited, but simply carrying out a job which had to be done. He placed the magnetized limpet mine on the hull of the ship, halfway between the keel and the Plimsoll line almost level with the engine-room—the most vulnerable place of all. He pulled at it, but it was so tight that he could not shift it. He swam away under water, until he was clear of the ship's wake, and surfaced. He then turned over on to his back, discarding his miniature oxygen cylinder, which would arouse suspicion if it was noticed. He had at least twenty minutes' grace, and had no idea that the harbour was now alive with men and boats searching for him. There was a slight risk of sharks, but he had a knife in his belt and sharks did not worry him. He was in no danger from the explosion, which should come just as the ship passed under Sydney Bridge.

Every frogman assigned to the emergency knew exactly what he had to do, and just how desperate the situation was. It would be almost impossible to prise off a limpet mine from the hull of the *Kookaburra*. It would have to be dismantled, a difficult and awkward task under water, and all the time they would work in the knowledge that if it exploded it would blow them to pieces.

First, *find* the bloody thing.

Six men on each side, they swam alongside the ship, those near the stern secured by lifeline against the pull of the propellor. They had to search the whole expanse of the red-painted hull and could not even be sure that a mine would be planted on the spot where a professional would place it. Fish swam close. Twice the long, grey shape of a shark passed near by as they worked.

Leading-frogman Kenneth Hallam was the first to see the round plate-like shape of the mine stuck to the side. He swam closer, made sure, and then released two smoke pellets which would rise to the surface and explode into white smoke when in contact with the air. Soon, others would come to his aid, but he had to start this job alone. He tried to prise it away, but as he had expected, it was stuck too tightly. The only hope was to dismantle it. Quite calmly, he began to prepare his tools.

Roger saw Luke Shaw in a larger launch only fifty yards away. His launch drew alongside, and he jumped from one to the other. For a moment he was dazzled by the sun, but he shaded his eyes and looked about him. Not far away was the Bridge, and the *Kookaburra* was swinging round perhaps fifty yards away from it. Next he saw the lifeboats being lowered into the water. The operation seemed to be taking place a long, long way from here. Reality was touched with unreality.

He joined Shaw in the thwarts.

Five minutes afterwards, two little clouds of smoke billowed up from the sea to the surface of the water.

"*See that?*" Shaw gasped. "They've found a mine."

"Luke," Roger said, "there's no point in any craft being too near unless it can be useful. Why don't you move your chaps back?"

"You going back?" demanded Shaw, almost truculently.

"No, but——"

"Be yourself," Shaw said brusquely.

They watched as the lifeboats pulled away, the ship slowed down almost to a standstill, dangerously close to the Bridge, the naval craft keeping close to the painted sides.

Ashore, police and naval and military units were moving bathers and surfers off the more exposed beaches. Blast could start a wave which could engulf the bays and carry death and destruction with it. Above, the Bridge was being closed to the annoyance of thousands of motorists. One piece of debris flung high by an explosion could carry disaster to any traffic on the broad highway.

Marcus Barring, still on his back, saw that the *Kookaburra* had virtually stopped, and was riding at anchor. He turned on his stomach and swam towards the nearest rocks, clambered on to them and stared across appalled by the sight of so many craft, the lifeboats, the evidence that the alarm had been raised.

"They got cold feet," he cried aloud. "The swine went chicken. I'll give them chicken."

Involuntarily, he touched the knife in his belt. Then he squatted and stared until gradually light began to glow in his eyes again. The *Kookaburra* was moving slowly away from the Bridge; very, very slowly.

"They'll never save her," he breathed. "They'll never save her. They haven't ten minutes left."

Two men had their heads close together, bodies diagonally away from each other, kicking to hold their position in the quiet water. Their fingers sometimes touched as one handed a tool to the other. The mine looked so innocent, just a big, thick, round plate on the side of the ship. One man drilled with professional care, knowing that if this mine had a booby trap there was no way to stop it from blowing them to pieces. The signal had gone out to all naval and police craft to move to points of safety. Luke Shaw was complaining bitterly about it; Roger only half heard him, he was so intent on the danger spot.

The two frogmen, one of them Hallam, could not, dared not hurry.

Once again the dark shape of a shark appeared, hovered, and moved sluggishly on.

A hush fell over the waiting, watching multitude on the ships, on the rocks, on the shore. The *Kookaburra* rode the calm waters with proud dignity. In the hearts of most men there was a prayer for success, in Marcus Barring's a fierce longing for the moment when the roar would come and smoke and water would hide the ship, then clear away and reveal her sinking.

The Master, with all his officers, was on the bridge. The

engineering officers and three ratings were in the engine room, taking the ship slowly away from the Bridge.

"I've never known anything worse," Luke muttered to Roger. "If we could only see what they're doing. From here it looks as if they aren't doing a bloody thing. I'd give a fortune to be on the job myself."

"I know what you mean," Roger said. "It would help if we knew how——"

A diver broke the surface of the water by the ship's side; a moment later another bobbed up. Luke put the glasses to his eyes, standing very still.

"Frogmen," he said, as if that wasn't obvious to the naked eye. "One of them's holding something in the air. He——"

There was a sudden outburst of cheering from the crew of the naval craft, and as it grew louder, the two frogmen began to swim towards it without any sense of urgency.

"Handsome," choked Luke Shaw. "They've made it."

He lowered the glasses, and then slowly and deliberately put out his right hand. As Roger gripped it, feeling almost weak with relief, Luke went on: "Now all we've got to do is find Barring and pin the job on to the Flags."

22

HATE KILLER

A MAN gave Roger a hand up as they reached Circular Quay. Sydney Cove was jammed tight with people, on the Manley Ferry terminal, on the Mosman Ferry terminal, by the ocean terminal, everywhere with a view of the quay. Two lifeboats from the *Kookaburra* were already near the landing-stage, someone raised a cheer.

A big man came up to Luke Shaw.

"Just had a message," he announced.

"Can't it wait?"

"Marcus Barring's been seen."

Roger caught his breath.

"Where?" demanded Shaw, softly.

"He was seen near the Yacht Club on the other side of the Bridge. He'd some goggles on at first, but took them off to put on his clothes. Before any of our chaps could reach him he'd disappeared."

"Any idea which way he was heading?"

"There's a report he was seen at Milson's Point Station, on the platform for the City trains."

Luke hesitated only for a moment. As he began to move, Roger said:

"Let's go." They piled into a waiting police car, and Luke ordered the driver:

"Ocean House, and make it a record."

"Okay."

"Handsome," Luke said, smacking his right hand on Roger's knee, "we saved that ship and all that's in it. My word, we did! I still can't believe the danger's over. Did you picture the same things as I did while we were waiting?"

"One big explosion," Roger said.

"The biggest! But it just didn't happen." Shaw proferred cigarettes. They lit up, and Shaw leaned back in his seat, still beaming. They could not make good speed because the traffic was so thick, and most of it seemed to be heading for the Cove. "Think any of the Flags will talk?" he asked.

"Gregory might."

"I know one way of making 'em," Luke said.

"What's that?"

"Let Marcus Barring get at them. They'd squeal all right."

"That's what we are doing, isn't it?"

"*What?*"

"You haven't warned your chaps to watch Ocean House yet."

"My word, I forgot it." Luke stretched over the empty seat in front of him and snatched the radio-phone from its hook. As soon as he heard a response, he boomed: "Charley, Marcus Barring's probably heading for Ocean House. If he gets there let him go up. Handsome West and I will be there in five minutes." He rang off, sat back, and beamed only a little less expansively. "You ever thought of retiring and becoming a private eye, Handsome?"

"Not yet. Why?"

"If you change your mind, let me know. We'll go into partnership." Shaw squashed out his cigarette on the floor, shot Roger a sideways glance, and went on: "I've got to admit there are advantages in having an organization behind you, though."

"Such as?" asked Roger. He spoke almost lazily, feeling a curious reaction of fatigue although he had not exerted himself physically. It was hard to realize the real weight of anxiety had gone, the nightmare of losing a ship with all hands had been banished. He hardly heard the beginning of Shaw's reply.

"You can get other people to do the chores for you, telephone London and other places."

"Telephone Lond——" Roger sat up. "Did you? Today?"

"Yes. To find out if there's any evidence Smith was a Communist. We got some very interesting information from your man Kebble, who was going to ring us, anyway. Smith wasn't a member of any Party, but he kept notes—doodling kind of notes. Kebble found an old notepad tucked away in a drawer. Some notes said: '*Expect call from Mr. Raymond, ten o'clock.*' Then there were doodles, the kind of thing you'd scribble while taking instructions from a boss. One note was: '*Imply attempt at take-over by Red C.?*'"

Roger had never been wider awake.

"See what that might mean," Luke said.

"I see. The Red take-over rumour started from Ocean House."

"That's what your man Kebble suggested. Bright boy, Kebble. If he ever wants to come to a land full of sunshine, I'll find him a job in the cop shop. Another note ran: '*£1000 for the B-Bs.*'"

"B-Bs—Barring Brothers!" Roger exclaimed.

"Who else? And Smith took a thousand quid in cash out of the bank that day."

"We've nearly got them," Roger said.

"You're right we have."

They were within sight of Ocean House, now, at the corner of Hunter Street and Spring.

"What else did you forget to tell me?" Roger demanded.

"I talked to Fred Hodges this morning, too. He's wormed a bit out of that Chinaman who nearly killed Doreen Morrison. The Chink was told to say he was a Commie and had orders from over the border, near Canton. Marcus Barring told him to say it. He didn't obey because he thought if he was a Red he'd be deported. He'd rather live in a Hong Kong jail. So the Barrings *and* the Flags spread the Red take-over story."

"Well, well," said Roger. "A very nice cover, and a very neat get out if any suspicions were aroused. The Flags employed the Barrings." He finished as the car drew up outside the skyscraper. A man sprang forward and opened the door.

"Barring arrived?"

"He was seen at the corner of Spring and Hunter a few minutes ago, sir."

"Let him come up," Shaw ordered.

"Right!"

A lift was waiting, almost as if it had been laid on for them. They stopped twice on the way to the top floor. The outer door of the Flag offices was ajar. Roger led the way. Raymond's secretary gave a startled smile, but before she spoke Shaw held out his card.

"Do you know Marcus Barring?"

"I have seen him, sir, yes."

"If he comes in let him go straight through to Mr. Raymond's office," Luke said.

"But Mr. Raymond said he wasn't to be disturbed."

"He wasn't expecting the police," Shaw retorted. As he went on, with Roger a step behind, he added in an aside: "She'll warn them, but it doesn't matter."

He opened the door of the Chairman's office as a telephone bell rang inside. Raymond Flag was at his desk, hand already on the telephone. Gregory was on the right, Mortimer on the left. They stared up at Roger, as if worked by strings. Raymond hesitated, and the bell kept on ringing.

"That's just to announce us," Luke Shaw said.

Mortimer sprang up. "You have no right to intrude like this."

"Yes, I know they are." Raymond put down the receiver slowly, and settled back in his chair. His poise was quite remarkable as he spoke.

"We are all tremendously relieved that the S.S. *Kookaburra* was not destroyed, or even damaged," he said. "We are glad to be able to congratulate you."

Gregory asked heavily: "Have you caught Barring?"

"We know where he is," Shaw stated flatly.

"Do you think he'll commit suicide like his brother did in London?" asked Roger.

"Or do you just hope?" mocked Luke.

"Unless you leave this office at once, I shall telephone the Commissioner of Police and lodge a complaint that you have continually exceeded your duty and have been rude to the point of insolence," Mortimer threatened. There was a pink tinge on his pale cheeks. "Go at once."

Neither Roger nor Luke Shaw moved. After a moment of tension, Mortimer stretched out his hand towards the telephone. Almost at once there were heavy footsteps outside, a woman's voice was raised—and the telephone rang, startling Mortimer so much that he snatched his hand away. Roger and Shaw moved back towards the wall which was flush with the door. Raymond reached out for the telephone, but before he could lift it the door burst open and Marcus Barring appeared. He strode in and slammed the door. Almost with the same movement he pulled his knife from the waistband of his jeans.

"So you told the police, you couldn't go through with it," he said raspingly. "I'm going to do what I ought to have done years ago—slit your throats instead of taking your filthy money."

He took another long stride forward. The three men in front of him seemed so petrified that they hardly remembered the two policemen.

Barring said to Mortimer: "You first, you fat slug, you started it. You——"

"What did he start?" inquired Luke Shaw, mildly.

Barring spun round towards him, knife in hand, already thrusting. Roger went forward smoothly and with hardly a sound, stretched out and grasped Barring's free hand, twisting so sharply that Barring gasped in pain. The fingers holding the knife grew slack. Shaw moved with almost casual speed, wrested the knife away, and tossed it on to the big desk. As it clattered, Roger pulled Barring round to face the directors, forcing the man's arm up behind him in a hammerlock.

"When you're talking to the Commissioner, Mr. Flag, tell him we also saved you from having your throats cut," Shaw said. "Then he'll really have it in for us."

"Barring," Roger said quietly, "did these men pay you to blow up the *Kookaburra*?"

"You bet they did!"

"Did they pay you and your brother to blow up the *Koala*?"

"Yes, the swine, they did."

"Did they order you to kill Sheldon and the others in London? And Sanderson in Hong Kong?"

"No one orders *me* about," Barring said roughly. "Sheldon

knew about the *Koala,* he was in on that deal. He knew about
the *Kookaburra,* too. He got cold feet and tried to stop us,
and——"

"You crazy liar!" Mortimer screamed at him. "I deny it,
we all deny every word. He hates our guts, he'd do anything to
destroy us."

"He's going to destroy you from the witness-box," Luke
Shaw said with supreme confidence. Roger had never heard
him speak so bitingly. "I am going to charge each one of you
with conspiracy to destroy a ship while at sea. That will do for
a start. Handsome, I expect some of my chaps followed
Barring up. Let 'em in, will you?"

When Roger let Barring go, the man made no attempt to
escape or to attack the Flags, just stood glaring at them as if
gloating over their downfall.

Roger left the police headquarters with Solomon Barring,
alias Ben Limm, about two hours later, and got into a police
car. The driver knew where to go, and Solomon knew that he
would soon be with Doreen. Now he relaxed in a corner as
Roger spoke.

"Your brother made a full confession, and I doubt if he left
much out. Both your brothers were thorns in the Flag flesh for
years, and Mortimer tried to buy them off. Two years ago the
Line was having a bad time. There were two successive years
of lower-than-average wool clip, and a recession which cut
imports sharply. The idea of sinking the *Koala* for insurance—
she was an old ship, over-insured—was attractive. It was to
have been done near land, without any lives lost. Marcus says
something went wrong with a timing mechanism of the limpet
mine, and the explosion was premature."

"I pray to God that's true," Solomon Barring said huskily.
"But the way they killed Denise and Sheldon—what made
them? What got into them?" He was in anguish because of his
brothers' crimes.

"Marcus says that Sheldon, who was party to the first

sinking, threatened to tell the whole story to the police if they
tried anything with the *Kookaburra*. Mortimer had asked him
to give extra insurance cover, he'd guessed why, and set out to
stop it. He hoped he could prevent the whole business without
paying for his part in the *Koala* disaster. We know what happened." He paused. "There was digitalis on board, and Paul
knew how to use a hypodermic syringe. We know what followed. Sheldon told your brothers that the two Morrison girls
and the First Engineer, Neil Sanderson, knew about the plot.
In London your brothers tried desperately to find out whether
they did know, for neither man wanted to kill the sisters.
Marcus and Denise had had an *affaire* on the outward voyage,
and Denise didn't mind continuing it on land. The 'Mr. and
Mrs. Brown' was false, of course, but there isn't much doubt
that Denise expected Marcus to marry her. Then his probing
questions made her suspicious, and there was a quarrel. Something she said made Marcus think Sheldon had told her, and
so Marcus killed her. Marcus hated the thought of killing
Doreen but there was so much at stake. The Flags had
promised them a ship of their own for a nominal sum."

"So it was for money," Solomon said heavily.

"Yes. The Flags bought the hatred out of your brothers,"
Roger said, "but evil remained in them. Sheldon found out
where they lived, and they frightened him into heading for
home. He swore he wouldn't talk to the police, but they didn't
think he would keep silent when he realized that Denise had
been murdered. So Paul watched London Airport, but wasn't
sure he used the digitalis in time—Sheldon went to a telephone booth unexpectedly. We know what happened afterwards."

"My own—brothers," Solomon said painfully.

"There was one good thing," Roger said. "Their fierce
family loyalty remained, and they would not injure you.
According to Marcus, Paul killed himself rather than be questioned and made to talk—he knew he would talk, he wasn't
one to hold out. I doubt if we'll ever know for certain why

Lancelot Smith killed himself. He was in the know about the *Koala* sinking, and it obviously tormented him."

"I think I can guess what happened," Solomon said. "I knew him well at one time. He had a deep sense of loyalty and would loathe any betrayal of trust. The crimes would prey on his mind, but he could not betray the Flags. He would never forget that in spite of his appearance they gave him that job in London." After a pause he went on: "Is there anything else?"

They were in the thick of the traffic at the end of Elizabeth Street now; thick, noisy traffic of which they were oblivious.

"The first indication of trouble was when your brother Paul received a note saying that someone on board the *Kookaburra* knew his part in the *Koala* sinking," Roger said. "He started to go through all the cabins, looking at handwriting, and he took an elderly passenger's wallet away, to search it. This was found in his cabin and he was dismissed for suspected theft. Marcus walked off with him. Strange man, your brother Marcus. When he switched allegiance to the Flags he was absolutely loyal until he thought they had failed him. As recently as last week he called them murdering swine and swore they wouldn't have a ship left, simply to try to draw my suspicions off them."

There was a film of tears in Solomon's eyes.

A minute later the car drew up outside the hotel. Roger saw Doreen Morrison on the steps of the hotel. As Solomon got out she came running, eyes glowing, arms outstretched, quite oblivious of the passing crowds.

"Drive me to the Wentworth," Roger said to the driver.

At least Solomon and Doreen would not take long to forget.

He was at the hotel foyer later that evening, when there was a telephone call for Mr. Jack Parrish. He saw a tall, handsome man get up from a table where he had been sitting with an attractive blonde ten or fifteen years younger. The way Jill Parrish watched her husband told Roger that their honeymoon was a long way from over.

He went up to his room later, and found a cable and a

letter; the letter from Janet. He opened the cable first and read:

> Congratulations from everyone including the Commander stop Sam Hackett married in Tours.
>
> Kebble.

Roger chuckled.

He opened Janet's letter, heart beating a little faster than normal, which was a remarkable thing for a man who had been married for nearly twenty-five years. The first sentence ran:

> "Darling, I'm so sorry about interrupting you at the airport, I haven't forgiven myself yet . . ."

He had barked at her—and *she* was apologizing. She remembered the incident so vividly but until this moment he had forgotten it. At least he need never tell her so.

> ". . . and you'll be an utter fool if you don't take at least a week of the leave the Yard owes you, to look at Australia. I'd hate you to miss that—much though I miss you.
> The boys say they'll write tomorrow. . . ."

Roger read the letter again, stepped to the window, saw traffic heading for the Bridge, the couples in the little park, the neon signs flashing; and in the distance, a glow of light in the harbour where the S.S. *Kookaburra* was tied up safe and sound.